A FOLLOWER CALLED MARK

THE CALLED
BOOK 11

KENNETH A. WINTER

WildernessLessons

JOIN MY READERS' GROUP FOR UPDATES AND FUTURE RELEASES

Please join my Readers' Group so i can send you a free book, as well as updates and information about future releases, etc.

See the back of the book for details on how to sign up.

A Follower Called Mark

The Called – Book 11 (a series of novellas)

Published by:

Kenneth A. Winter

WildernessLessons, LLC

Richmond, Virginia

United States of America

kenwinter.org

wildernesslessons.com

The Called is a registered trademark of Kenneth A. Winter.

Edited by Sheryl Martin Hash

Cover design by Scott Campbell Design

ISBN 978-1-9568663-7-7(softcover)

ISBN 978-1-9568663-8-4(e-book)

ISBN 978-1-9568663-9-1 (large print)

Library of Congress Control Number: 2024908643

The basis for the storyline of this book is taken from *the Gospel according to Mark* and *the Acts of the Apostles* in the Holy Bible. Certain fictional events or depictions of those events have been added.

DEDICATION

To my friend, Joshua

❧

As iron sharpens iron, so a friend sharpens a friend.
Proverbs 27:17

❧

CONTENTS

PREFACE

~

This fictional novella is the eleventh book in the series titled, *The Called*. Like the others, it is a story about an ordinary person who surrendered his life to God and was called by Him to be used in extraordinary ways. As i've said in my previous books, we tend to elevate the people we read about in Scripture and place them on a pedestal far beyond our reach because of the faith they exhibited. But Mark would tell us that he was a flawed human being who could never have accomplished on his own what God did through him.

In that respect, his story is very similar to mine . . . and probably yours. There were times in his life when he impetuously made wrong decisions, but there were others when he chose to follow God in obedience. For example, we have the Gospel according to Mark. However, God would have orchestrated for us to have the Gospel according to someone else had Mark been disobedient. It was never about Mark's ability; rather, it was about his availability.

The storyline is, of course, taken from the Gospel according to Mark, the Book of Acts, and numerous epistles written by the apostles Paul and

Peter in the Holy Bible. Mark is notorious for having abandoned Barnabas and Paul two months into their missionary journey. Whether Barnabas was correct when he invited Mark to join him and Paul on their planned second journey, or if Paul was correct in refusing to allow him to go, is the topic of much discussion.

That event, together with so many others in the life of Mark—or John Mark as he is often referred to in the Bible—unfold in this story. Little is known about John Mark prior to that fateful first missionary journey, but there is much that can be inferred based on two events recorded in Scripture.

The first is what most scholars agree is his cameo appearance in the Gospel he penned as recorded in Mark 14:51-52. The second is the apparent financial standing of his mother—indicated by the size of her home and her employment of household servants—recorded in Acts 12:12-17. (I suggest reading those two passages before you begin reading the story.)

In writing this book, i have taken what we know about John Mark from Scripture and crafted a plausible story that provides insight into what his life may have been like. So, i invite you to join John Mark as he shares his unique story and the stories of three men— Barnabas, Paul, and Peter— who were instrumental in his life. You will recognize many of the other individuals mentioned as well; i have created background details for some so we might better see them as people and not just names.

i have also added several fictional characters to round out the story, plus i have given names to those we know existed but remained unnamed in the Bible. They represent people who would have surrounded John Mark during his lifetime. Included as an appendix in the back of this book is a character listing to clarify the historical vs. fictional elements of each character.

Whenever i directly quote Scripture, it is italicized and includes a super-script number. The Scripture references are also included as an appendix in the book. The remaining instances of dialogue not italicized are a part of the fictional story that helps advance the narrative.

My hope is this book will prompt you to reread the biblical accounts of John Mark's life and the events surrounding it. You will be reminded of how God worked through this ordinary man to accomplish His extraordinary purpose. None of my books is intended to be a substitute for God's Word; rather, i hope they will lead you to spend more time in His Word.

Finally, my prayer is you will see John Mark through fresh eyes and be challenged to live out *your* walk with the Lord with the same conviction, courage, and faith he displayed. And most importantly, i pray you will be challenged to be an "ordinary" follower with the willingness and faith to be used by God in extraordinary ways—to impact not only this generation, but also the generations to come . . . until our Lord returns!

1

GETHSEMANE

∽

I was jolted awake by a loud commotion. Concerned, I peered through the bushes surrounding my hiding spot. It was still pitch black, but I could make out a large group of men with torches advancing up the path from the city.

"There they are, just up ahead!" one of them yelled.

Surely, this boisterous crowd was not seeking Jesus or His disciples at this time of night! As they drew closer, I realized the throng included Roman soldiers, temple guards, priests, and other men carrying clubs. Then, the face of the man who appeared to be the leader came into focus. It was Judas Iscariot!

What did they want? Was Judas leading these men to come protect Jesus?

I did my best to stay hidden as they passed by. If word got back to my mother I had spent the night in the Garden of Gethsemane, she would certainly be angry. I hadn't really planned to stay this long. I was just curious about what Jesus and His disciples were going to do, so I followed them. Unfortunately, I fell asleep.

Apparently, Jesus's disciples had been sleeping too, but they quickly roused as the soldiers unsheathed their swords. Fear crossed the disciples' faces when temple guards threatened them with their spears and other men brandished their clubs. It became obvious this mob was not here to protect Jesus!

"Centurion, tell a few of your men to remain here with these," Judas called out. "Jesus is farther up the hill. The rest of you follow me as I approach Him."

I glanced up the knoll and spotted Peter, James, and John standing a short distance from Jesus.

Judas walked up to Him and loudly exclaimed, *"Rabbi!"*[1] He greeted Jesus with a kiss—as if he hadn't seen the Master in a long time—though they had been together earlier that night at supper. Judas was extending a formal greeting for a respected teacher and mentor in contrast to the way Jesus and the disciples usually greeted one another.

"Judas, would you betray the Son of Man with a kiss?"[2] Jesus responded.

Betray! I couldn't believe my ears! Judas was one of Jesus's closest disciples. He had been entrusted with managing the treasury of Jesus and the disciples—as meager as it was. Surely he wasn't seeking to harm the Lord!

But what happened next confirmed my worst suspicions. The captain of the guard told the temple guards to arrest Jesus. A man standing near the Lord acted like he was going to swing his club at the Master. Peter immediately drew his sword against the man and struck him on the right side of his head. I'll never forget the sound of that man's blood-curdling scream.

Jesus looked at His disciples and shouted, *"No more of this! Put away your sword. Don't you realize that I could ask My Father for thousands of angels to protect us, and He would send them instantly?"*[3]

Then I witnessed the most miraculous sight. Jesus reached out and touched the wounded man's ear. Immediately, the man felt the side of his head and realized Jesus had healed him. He dropped his club and knelt before the Lord.

The disciples began to scatter in different directions. Peter and John ran up the mount, while the rest scurried down the hill away from the city. I couldn't believe the disciples were abandoning Jesus! *What should I do? How could I possibly help Jesus?* I looked around and discovered I was the only one left on the mount with Him.

What would the mob do if they spotted me? Would they arrest me? I panicked and decided to run. But in my haste, I failed to see the Roman soldier standing nearby and crashed right into him.

"What have we here?" he asked with a menacing snarl as he grabbed me by the back of my tunic. "A boy hiding in the bushes! Where do you think you are going, boy? The others seem to have gotten away, but you're not going to escape so easily!"

A burst of adrenaline gave me additional strength, and I kicked the soldier in the shin as hard as I could. Caught by surprise, he momentarily loosened his grip, providing me with an opportunity to escape. With the soldier still holding on, my tunic ripped at the seam, and I literally ran out of my clothes. I did not care I was running naked down the hill. All I knew was I needed to get far away from that place and that mob.

Eventually, I realized no one was pursuing me; Jesus must be the only one they were interested in. I was immediately overwhelmed by the reality of what I had done. Just like His trusted disciples, I also had deserted Jesus. I had followed Him up the hill because I wanted to be one of His disciples. But instead of standing by His side, I had run away in fear.

I fell to my knees and wept in shame. After a while, I realized I needed to get home before the sun came up. I decided to sneak back up the hill to look for my clothing. The garden was abandoned except for my torn tunic lying in the path.

I quickly put it on as best I could and headed home. I may have escaped the soldiers, but I would not escape my mother's wrath. However, that was the least of my concerns at the moment. Jesus's followers must quickly be alerted to what had taken place, and my mother would know what to do. The religious leaders had not hidden their hatred for Jesus. There was no imagining what they were planning to do next!

~

2

THERE MUST BE SOME MISTAKE!

~

*I*t was still dark when I arrived home. As I quietly made my way through the door in the gate, I noticed candlelight shining from my mother's room. She was obviously waiting up for me.

None of the servants were stirring as I hurriedly went to tell her what had happened to Jesus.

Before she had the opportunity to ask me where I had been, I blurted out, "They've arrested Jesus!"

"What do you mean, John Mark?" my mother asked. (She always calls me John Mark when she is upset with me). "Who's arrested Jesus?"

"A group of Roman soldiers, priests, and temple guards surrounded Him in the Garden of Gethsemane a little while ago and took Him away! And they were being led by Judas Iscariot!"

"Well, if Judas was leading them, they couldn't possibly have been arresting Jesus," my mother countered. "You must have misinterpreted what you saw."

"Mother, you don't understand. Peter and all the other disciples ran away in fear. There is no question He was being arrested."

"For what reason?" my mother asked skeptically. "Jesus hasn't done anything that would warrant His arrest. There must be some mistake! And why would Judas have been leading them? Where did Peter and the others go?"

"I don't know."

"We must find out what has happened," she continued, speaking more to herself than to me. "Who would possibly know? Oh, I know! The pharisee —Joseph of Arimathea! He is a member of the Sanhedrin and has secretly become a follower of Jesus. If anyone knows, he will.

"Mark, run to his home. Tell him what has happened and find out what he knows."

"Should I disturb him this early?"

"If something has happened to Jesus, he will want to know," Mother said, "regardless of the hour. Time is of the essence. Run quickly to his home . . . and later you can tell me why you were at the Garden of Gethsemane at this hour!"

I changed into another tunic and ran as fast as I could. The members of the Sanhedrin—who had come to Jerusalem from other parts of Judea and from Galilee in order to serve—all lived in an enclave in the upper city. I was familiar with Joseph's home because my mother and I had accompanied the disciple John on a visit there several months earlier. That's when we discovered Joseph had become a follower of Jesus.

As John and Joseph discussed Jesus that night, I had learned that John was a former student at the school of the highly respected Rabbi Hillel. Since most pharisees had also sat under Hillel's tutelage, they seemed comfortable asking John questions about Jesus. John had brought my mother along since numerous followers in Jerusalem were gathering at our home for weekly prayer. Although Joseph had not been attending, he discreetly began coming to the prayer meetings a few weeks later.

I began pounding on Joseph's door.

"How dare you knock on my master's door at this hour!" an irate servant reprimanded me. "Go away! The household is still sleeping—just as you should be!"

"But it's important that I see your master now," I replied. "Tell him Mary's son, John Mark, is at his door with an urgent message about Jesus."

The servant's demeanor softened as soon as I mentioned Jesus, and she reluctantly agreed to wake her master. I was promptly allowed to enter and wait for Joseph. Within moments, he appeared wearing his sleeping garment.

"What's your urgent message about Jesus, John Mark?"

I quickly explained everything that had occurred at the Garden of Gethsemane.

"This is the work of Annas and Caiaphas!" Joseph exclaimed. "You did right to bring this information to me. Let me see what I can find out. Go back and tell your mother to call upon Jesus's followers to pray. I will send word as soon as I have more information."

Within the hour, I had assisted my mother in alerting followers in Jerusalem to gather at our home for prayer. The sun was peeking above the horizon as we began to pray for the protection of Jesus.

Shortly thereafter, a messenger arrived with word from Joseph. His message read: "The Sanhedrin has falsely accused Jesus of blasphemy and charged Him with acts of sedition. He is to be tried before Pontius Pilate. They intend to convince Pilate to have Jesus crucified. Pray that cooler heads will prevail, and Pilate will realize this is all madness."

I told my mother I could not hide in our home while Jesus was being falsely accused. I must go to the courtyard outside the praetorium.

"Your efforts will be much better spent here, my son, lifting your voice and heart in prayer for the Father's intercession," my mother replied. "What influence can you possibly have over what is happening at the praetorium?"

"Probably none," I admitted. "But at least, I will be there near Him . . . and will not have abandoned Him!"

I was nearly in tears as I spoke, and my mother sensed what was in my heart.

"Go to where He is then," she said, "but do not do anything rash."

By the time I arrived at the praetorium, Jesus had already been sentenced to death. The spectators that remained were discussing how Jesus had been taken to the Antonia Fortress. I quickly made my way there.

I saw a cohort of Roman soldiers exiting the fortress. In their midst were three men, each carrying a cross. I prayed that Jesus was not one of them. I worked my way through the crowd to get a closer look. When I was within arm's length of one of the soldiers, I studied each prisoner's face. I gasped when I saw the third man.

It was Jesus! His face had been pummeled, and He was barely recognizable. He wore a crown of thorns that had been thrust into His scalp. Blood was streaming down His face and neck. I cried out in horror at how viciously He had been beaten.

The soldier closest to me shouted, "Be quiet, you!" I never saw the club he was wielding until it made contact with the side of my head. Suddenly everything went dark as I fell to the ground.

3

CYPRUS

~

*M*y grandfather, Andros, grew up in the coastal city of Paphos in southwest Cyprus. After the demise of the Roman Republic, Cyprus became a senatorial province of the newly constituted empire during the reign of Emperor Augustus. Once the political upheaval subsided, Cyprus began to enjoy a prosperous economy.

While still a young man, my grandfather became interested in the profitable trade of olive oil. Historically, presses had been situated in the rural portions of Cyprus, which satisfied the local need for olive oil. However, Andros knew greater profits could be made by exporting Cypriot oil to other parts of the empire along the coast of the Mediterranean Sea. Even though the growers would have to transport their olives a little farther to the city, Andros compensated them for their efforts. He then delivered large quantities of freshly pressed oil to the cargo holds of merchant ships in port.

My grandfather quickly became the leading exporter of Cypriot olive oil and profited greatly. He soon rose in station to become one of the prominent citizens of Paphos. Andros lived in a grand home that overlooked the sea, second only in size and grandeur to that of the provincial governor. My father, Damaris, grew up enjoying the privileges of wealth and was trained by my grandfather in the art of increasing the family fortune.

One day my father met a beautiful, young Jewish woman named Mary, the daughter of a successful merchant. As their budding relationship grew, Mary often talked about her desire to return to her childhood home of Jerusalem. Since my father knew Jerusalem was situated a long distance from any seaport, he had no interest in relocating—but he did have a great interest in Mary!

Love won out, and the two soon married. My father hoped their new life together would diminish Mary's yearning to return to Jerusalem. But that was not the case. Even my birth, one year later, did nothing to change her mind. If anything, her desire for me to grow up in her childhood home only strengthened her resolve. My father soon acknowledged that if he were going to enjoy a life of marital bliss, he would have to explore a way for them to live in Jerusalem.

My grandfather approached my father with a solution. "The answer to the problem is salt!" he exclaimed with delight.

"Salt?" my father replied dubiously. "How could that possibly provide a solution?"

"In order to live in Jerusalem," my grandfather explained, "you need a reliable source of income. Since the city is not situated near a port and is not a large-scale producer of exportable goods, you must look at something else. What is the city known for?"

"The Jewish Temple is located in Jerusalem," my father replied. "Three times each year, the Jews make a pilgrimage there to worship their Hebrew God. They bring their sacrifices and offerings to the Temple, and the most prosperous trades all center around that activity."

"That is correct, my son! And one of the products they greatly need is salt. It is sprinkled on their sacrifices to show their trust in their God—and used in massive quantities during the festivals. It is also used in large supply in Galilee as a preservative for the fish harvested from the sea. The salted fish is then exported throughout the Roman Empire.

"One of our best olive oil customers in Sicily is looking to make a trade for salt. His salt, considered by many to be of the finest quality, could easily be brought to the port in Caesarea Maritima and from there distributed to Galilee and Jerusalem. You could become the premier salt importer and distributor for that region."

"But why do they need to import salt?" my father asked. "Don't they already harvest more than they need from the Dead Sea?"

"Perhaps," my grandfather replied with a smile. "But the salt from the Dead Sea has a bitter taste of which everyone complains. The salt you import will provide them with the solution they are seeking!"

And that is what prompted my father to move my mother and me to Jerusalem. Within a short time, he became very successful in his new business venture and was soon recognized as one of Jerusalem's principal merchants. Though he was not a devout Jew, my father knew that to be recognized as a leader in the community he must be seen regularly in the Court of the Gentiles of the Temple.

When I turned five years old, my parents decided I should attend yeshiva school. From then until I was ten years old, the only book from which I was taught was the Tanakh—made up of the Law of Moses (the Torah), the words of the Prophets (the Nevi'im), and the poetic books (the Ketuvim).

The year I was nine, my father came home with surprising news at the beginning of Passover.

"A Man entered the Temple today. He had a handful of disciples following Him, so He appeared to be a rabbi. At first, I thought He was a mad man.

"He was using a whip made of rope to chase the priests and merchants out of the outer court, driving their animals with them, and turning over their tables and stalls. I heard the Man shout to the priests, *'Get these things out of here. Stop turning My Father's house into a marketplace!'*[1]

"'What are You doing?' the priests retorted. 'Who gave You authority to come in here and do this? This is the Temple of Jehovah God. Only those under His authority can make such demands. If Your authority comes from Him, then show us a miraculous sign to prove it!'

"The Man replied, *'All right. Destroy this Temple, and in three days I will raise it up.'*

"'What!' they exclaimed in exasperation. *"It has taken forty-six years to build this Temple, and You can rebuild it in three days?*[2] You must be mad!'

"But the Man did not answer. He simply stared at them. One by one, the priests cleared the area and moved everything to the pavilions and storage pens outside the Temple walls. It was as if they knew they had been doing wrong, and someone had finally called them on it. The Man continued to watch them.

"I was amazed that although He showed righteous indignation toward the priests, He never lost control. Actually, He seemed very much in control. Even His anger was different from anything I had ever witnessed. And I kept thinking about His statement. What did He mean when He said, *'Destroy this Temple, and in three days I will raise it up'*?[3]

"After the priests were finished, the Man stayed in the Court of the Gentiles and I learned His name was Jesus of Nazareth. He began to teach from the Scriptures to those of us gathered. His teaching was unlike any I had ever heard. He spoke with authority and understanding. Initially, people were drawn to Him because of his power over the priests and merchants, but the crowd grew as we all marveled at His teaching."

~

4

IN THE COURTYARD OF THE TEMPLE

~

*T*he next day, my mother and I accompanied my father to the Temple to listen to Jesus. My parents remarked throughout the day how His teaching spoke to their hearts. However, my attention was captivated by the miracles He performed.

We watched as a father carried his young son, who appeared to be half my age, up to Jesus. The father explained the boy had been injured when he was a toddler and had not been able to walk since.

"Teacher," the man pleaded, "I have heard You have the ability to make the lame to walk. Would you please heal my son?"

Jesus looked at them with compassion—first the father, then the son. He looked back at the father and asked, "Do you believe that I can?"

"Yes, Teacher, I do!" the man answered immediately.

Jesus replied, "Then set your son down upright on his two legs."

To his credit, the father didn't hesitate . . . and neither did the boy.

"Father, there is strength in my legs!" the boy cried out. He took several steps and shouted, "I can feel it. Father, I can walk!"

Tears streamed down the father's cheeks as he thanked Jesus. Everyone in the crowd was amazed as the father and son left hand in hand, with the boy skipping as he walked.

We witnessed the miracle of healing time and again that day. Though people's maladies varied, the result was always the same—complete healing. And the crowd was astonished each time!

My father and mother turned to each other at one point and declared, "He is the Messiah! He can be no other."

A little later, I heard them discussing the reaction of the priests and religious leaders.

"Why aren't they here declaring Jesus is the One for whom we have waited? Surely, they must realize who He is. Why do they just stare at Him from a distance?"

My father noticed a small group of Galilean men and women who remained close to Jesus throughout the day.

"Those same men and women were near Him yesterday," my father told my mother. "They must be His disciples. We should go introduce ourselves, and see if they can tell us more about Jesus."

One of the men turned toward us as we approached and quietly greeted my father.

"Peace be upon you," he said, as he extended his hand in greeting. "My name is Andrew, son of Jonah. I remember seeing you here yesterday. I see you brought companions today. Is this your wife and son?"

"Yes, this is my son, John Mark, and my wife, Mary."

"Peace be upon you both," Andrew replied, nodding at us. Then, addressing my father, he asked, "What brings you back today?"

"I am not a devout Jew" my father acknowledged, "but Jesus speaks like no other I have heard. His words penetrate our hearts, and we are moved by the compassion He extends as He heals the sick. Where does He come from?"

"Those of us who are here with Him, have only been traveling with Him for a short while," Andrew replied. "We, too, have been moved by His words and actions. He was raised as a carpenter in Galilee, but He is so much more than that. We believe Him to be the Messiah who's coming was foretold, but He has not revealed that to us—at least, not yet."

"How did it come about that you began to follow Him?" my father asked.

"A number of us are fishermen from Galilee, and for a while several of us were disciples of John the baptizer. One day, Jesus appeared at the Jordan River and asked John to baptize Him. The rest of us didn't pay much attention, but John knew who He was from the moment He arrived. But as quickly as He came, He departed. And none of us was the wiser.

"Six weeks later, however, He returned to the river after spending time in the wilderness. He didn't come to speak to anyone; rather, He just continued to walk by the water. It was then that the baptizer announced to my friend, also named John, and me, '*Look! There is the Lamb of God!*'[1]

"We didn't know what that meant, but my friend and I knew we needed to follow Him. So we joined Jesus and have been with Him ever since. Our number has now grown. That fellow standing over there is a shepherd from Bethlehem named Shimon. He set out with us that first day and is the only one of us who is not a Galilean.

"Later, those two standing beside Shimon joined us. Philip and Bartholomew are also fishermen from my hometown. The man on the other side of them was another one of the baptizer's disciples—a former zealot named Simon. The next two men are Jesus's cousins, carpenters named James and Thaddeus. And lastly, the two women joining our ranks, to keep a motherly eye on us, are my mother, Salome, and Jesus's aunt Mary, the mother of James and Thaddeus.

"We have all been drawn to Jesus from the moment we first met Him, and we all know we have much to learn from Him and about Him."

"Where are you staying while you are in Jerusalem?" my mother inquired.

"The past two nights we slept in the Gethsemane Garden on the Mount of Olives," Andrew answered. "Jesus enjoys going to the garden to pray, and though we try to stay awake and pray with Him, we most often fall asleep."

"Why don't you all come and stay with us while you are here?" my mother replied. "We have plenty of space, and we would consider it a privilege."

My father gave my mother a look of surprise, but soon he was nodding his head in agreement and encouraging Andrew to answer yes.

"That is most kind of you," Andrew said. "Please allow me to ask the Master when He finishes teaching what He plans to do this evening."

Shortly thereafter, Jesus told the crowd it was time for Him to rest, and He challenged them to consider what He had taught them. "If the Father wills, I will be back here tomorrow," Jesus said as He left and walked toward us.

Andrew leaned in and softly spoke to Him. Jesus smiled at my family and said, "Yes, of course we will stay with Damaris and Mary tonight. The Father told me to expect their invitation."

"Come My friends," He called out as He beckoned to the rest of our group. "Lead the way! There is much for us to talk about."

5

HOME

~

I felt so honored to be in Jesus's presence as my parents and I led His contingent through the streets of Jerusalem to our home. Even as a nine-year-old boy, I knew Jesus was like no other. Though I did not fully understand what my parents meant when they called Him the Messiah, I knew my people had long awaited the arrival of someone special.

Jesus paused speaking to my parents and addressed me. "John Mark, what do you think about what you saw and heard this afternoon?" His question caught me completely off guard.

As I looked up into His eyes, I sensed He could see into my very soul. I somehow knew there was no secret I could keep from Him and nothing about me He didn't already know. But rather than feel threatened by those thoughts, I was actually calmed by them.

It also surprised me that Jesus remembered my name. I had long ago learned that adults don't pay much attention to children—unless the adult is a family member or a teacher—and even then, the attention is often limited. But Jesus seemed intently interested in hearing my thoughts.

"Well," I haltingly began, "I have never seen anyone do the things You do. You made the lame to walk and the blind to see! I think You must have been sent by God."

"Then you have seen more clearly than many of the religious leaders, John Mark," Jesus replied. Turning to the rest of the group, He said, *"Anyone who welcomes a little child like this one on My behalf welcomes Me, and anyone who welcomes Me welcomes My Father who sent Me."*[1]

When we arrived home, my mother and the servants hurriedly set about preparing a meal for our guests. My father welcomed Jesus with a kiss on both cheeks and the traditional greeting, "This is Your house." A servant brought water to wash the dust off our guests' feet before everyone reclined around our table.

Jesus taught us throughout the evening. Most of the Scriptures He used were ones I had learned at school, but I found His explanations were much clearer and more concise than those of my teachers. To be honest, I often struggled to understand my teachers' lessons.

By the end of the evening, my parents and all our servants proclaimed they were believers. I, too, expressed my belief in Him. In light of what Jesus had said earlier about children, no one protested my declaration.

Jesus taught in the Temple courtyard the next two days and stayed with us both nights. My older cousin Joseph joined us the second night. He was the son of my mother's older brother and had come from Cyprus to study under Rabbi Gamaliel. He also assisted my father in the salt business as his studies permitted.

Joseph had heard about Jesus from my father and wanted to come see and hear for himself. He listened intently to Jesus's teachings and before the evening was over, he also professed himself to be a believer.

On the third and final night Jesus was with us, He led those who had expressed their faith in Him to the mikveh pools adjacent to the Temple. His disciples baptized us as a ceremonial cleansing of our sins.

Jesus told us, *"You are the light of the world—like a city on a hilltop that cannot be hidden. No one lights a lamp and then puts it under a basket. Instead, a lamp is placed on a stand, where it gives light to everyone in the house. In the same way, let your good deeds shine out for all to see, so that everyone will praise your heavenly Father."* [2]

As Jesus and His entourage departed Jerusalem the next morning, everyone in my household regretted we were not going too. But Jesus told us He needed us to remain in Jerusalem and shine our lights in the Temple and throughout the city.

"Wait here for My return," He instructed, "and observe all I have taught you." Gratefully, Jesus returned multiple times for the observance of our religious festivals. Each time He did, our hearts quickened.

The following autumn, my father announced that he needed to travel to Sicily to meet with his salt supplier. Trade in Jerusalem and Galilee had continued to grow, and my father required additional supply to meet demand. He would sail from Caesarea Maritima to Paphos and from there to Sicily.

I begged my father to take me with him, and finally he relented. It would be my first opportunity to visit our homeland of Cyprus, meet our many relatives there, and travel to Sicily. I was beyond excited!

My father and I set out on the backs of donkeys through the rugged terrain of Judea, passing through small villages and towns along the way. As we approached the coast, we arrived at the port city of Caesarea Maritima. Though I had traveled through the city when we first arrived in this country, I was too young to remember it. I was awed by the grand architecture of the city built by King Herod the Great.

We boarded one of the ships my father used to transport his goods. Like most merchant ships, it was built with a broad, flat bottom and a rounded hull—which made it suitable for navigating both the shallow waters near the coast as well as the open seas.

A single mast with a large square sail jutted out of the deck. The ship's captain told my father that favorable winds and a smooth sea would have us in Paphos within a matter of days.

By the second day of sailing, I was struck by the vastness and beauty of the Mediterranean. It reminded me of just how big the world is and how the seas connect us all. As we entered the bustling harbor of Paphos, I admired the dance of fishing boats and merchant ships as they came and went.

Sunlight glinted off the stone buildings lining the water's edge. The city offered a cacophony of seagulls squawking, ship masts creaking, boat hulls banging against rocks, and the distant hum of the market. The aroma of food, spices, and the distinct fragrances of the Mediterranean teased my senses. I quickly discovered I was hungry.

As we prepared to disembark, my father pointed to an older man on the dock giving instructions to the crew of another vessel. "That's your grandfather, John Mark."

～

6

A SHORT VISIT IN PAPHOS

~

I could not get over how much my father and grandfather looked alike. They both had hair and eyes as dark as ebony, with olive skin that had been bronzed by years in the sun. The two shared the same height and build; apart from their age difference, they easily could have been mistaken for one another. I, however, looked nothing like them, with the exception of my dark hair and eyes. I possessed my mother's fair complexion and a much slighter build.

I will never forget my grandfather's greeting as my father and I approached him. He wrapped his arms around both of us and gave us the biggest embrace I'd ever received. I thought my ribs would be crushed, but thankfully he relaxed his grip as he studied each of us.

"Why didn't you tell us you were coming, Damaris?"

"I wanted to surprise you, Papa," my father replied, smiling. "And I wanted you to see your grandson again before he gets any older."

"Well, you have definitely surprised me! And your mother will be beside herself with joy!"

He then introduced us to the crew on the dock.

"Damaris, this is Artemis, captain of the finest merchant ship to ever navigate the seas—the Kyrenia. He is preparing to set sail in three days with a full cargo of our olive oil bound for Sicily."

"Captain Artemis, it is a pleasure to meet you," my father said. "My son and I may have interest in sailing with you. Do you have room for us?"

My grandfather interrupted before the captain had a chance to reply. "Surely, you would not leave us so soon, Damaris! Your mother and I will want you to spend more time with us."

"Yes, Papa, I know. And John Mark and I want to spend more time with you, but I have business in Sicily. Perhaps I can sail there on the Kyrenia, conduct my business, and return here with them."

Captain, what about it?" my father asked. "Do you have space for me and my son?"

"Yes, I would be honored to have the son and grandson of my dear friend join us—if your father agrees," the captain replied. He obviously did not want to risk offending my grandfather.

"Then it's settled," my grandfather replied. "They will sail with you in three days, and then you will bring them back to us!"

I didn't think it possible, but my grandmother's greeting eclipsed my grandfather's when we arrived at their home! Over the next three days, my grandparents introduced me to more relatives than I could imagine—on my mother's side as well as my father's. I was grateful I had a mind for details and the ability to remember everyone's name.

The days passed quickly, and soon we were back at the dock boarding the Kyrenia. Captain Artemis told us it should take sixteen days to reach Syracusae on the coast of Sicily.

The ship's crew was comprised of six men in addition to the captain. Four of the men, including the helmsman named Zafer, had sailed with the captain for over ten years. The other two, including the cook, had recently joined the crew. All of them were quite proficient, and my father had to admit that the Kyrenia was one of, if not the best, merchant ship to ever set sail.

The skies were clear, and the seas were calm the first few days of our mid-September voyage. However, on our fifth day we began encountering high waves and strong winds from the southeast. The captain informed us this weather was unusual for this time of year.

Before the day was done, the winds had increased to typhoon strength and the waves were breaking above the ship's bow. The captain and crew looked concerned. We were a day away from the closest harbor on the island of Crete—and the wind and seas were now working against us.

Soon torrential rain and hail pelted the deck. The captain gave the order to strike the sails and batten down the ship. The rough swells tossed us about since the water was too deep for the ship's anchors to take hold. My father and I helped the crew band the ship with heavy ropes to strengthen the hull.

My father continued to assure me we would be all right, but I could tell he was worried. We both heard Captain Artemis tell his crew he had never seen a storm this bad.

When morning broke, the storm was still raging. But everyone was encouraged when one of the sailors announced he could see land in the distance. The crew began to take depth soundings; the water was now thirty meters deep. The captain instructed the men to set the foresail and rudder in place so he could attempt to steer the ship toward shore. Suddenly, the ship struck rocks hidden below the surface.

The bow splintered and the entire ship shook as an ill-timed wave sent three men overboard including my father!

Fierce waves battered the men as the tide pushed them farther away from our sinking ship. Captain Artemis shouted for the crew to lower the lifeboat.

"Hold on, Father! They're coming for you!" I cried out in desperation.

The ship's stern abruptly came about in the waves, smashing the lifeboat against the rocks; all that remained were pieces of splintered wood. I was terrified. *How are we going to rescue my father?* The captain told the remaining crew to abandon ship and told me to remain by his side.

Once we were submerged in water, the captain strapped me to a piece of the broken ship to keep me afloat. He directed Zafer to do the same and to stay with me while Captain Artemis swam off to rescue my father. I shouted for my father over and over, but I could hear nothing over the roar of the storm. Zafer advised me to conserve my energy since we did not have enough stamina to reach land.

At that moment, I realized my father was gone. Paralyzing grief, terror, and shock overwhelmed me. As our situation deteriorated, I suspected we all would soon face a similar fate. The storm continued to rage throughout the day and into the night, only adding to my desperation.

I began to shiver uncontrollably as the temperatures fell. I was exhausted, and my body was demanding sleep, but Zafer kept urging me to stay awake.

"If you fall asleep, you will slip below the water," he told me. Even in the midst of my grief, I sensed my father urging me to hold on.

Although I thought the night would never end, eventually the sun did dawn, and the wind and waves calmed. Fortunately, the current had pushed us closer to shore. With what little strength we had left, Zafer and I swam the rest of the way. By midday we made it to dry land—Zafer, the cook, two other members of the crew, and me. As we looked back out to sea, there were no signs of the Kyrenia and its cargo—everything was lost.

And it was painfully apparent that my father, Captain Artemis, and two members of the crew had perished in the storm. Tears of sorrow flooded my soul.

∽

7

THE JOURNEY BACK TO CYPRUS

~

*T*he survivors rested for a short while before Zafer took charge and directed us to start walking westward along the shoreline. He believed we were near the coastal city of Hierapytna. We were all grateful when he proved to be correct; the five of us arriving at the city gates around dusk.

"This city once boasted a large fleet of pirate ships," Zafer explained to me. "Merchant ships like ours maintained a safe distance from its shores, but still, many fell prey. One of the reasons the Romans conquered this island was to suppress that activity. Rome had no interest in sharing its financial gains with a group of marauders.

"Today, however, the city prospers as a waypoint for Mediterranean trade. We'll be able to find a ship to take us back to Paphos and get you safely back to your grandparents."

As we surveyed the harbor, Zafer spotted a ship that bore Cypriot markings. Its captain knew the Kyrenia and Captain Artemis well and expressed his sympathy for our loss. He especially tried to comfort me when he learned my father had died in the wreck. He confided that when he was about my age, his father had died in a tragic accident. It was clear he understood how I was feeling.

"We will set sail for Salamis, on the east side of the island of Cyprus, in two days," he told us. "You are all welcome to come with us, and we can drop you off at Paphos along the way. In the meantime, you can lodge with us here in Hierapytna. It won't be the finest place you've ever stayed, but it won't be the worst."

Once the five of us settled in our rooms, we immediately fell asleep. The sun was high in the sky when I awoke the next day. By then, most of the city's residents had heard about our situation. The sympathetic innkeeper told us he had set aside some of that morning's food to ensure we had breakfast.

After a good night's rest and a satisfying meal, I felt much stronger—emotionally and physically. In fact, I told the innkeeper I felt as if I had stayed in a palace. His reaction told me I had paid him the ultimate compliment. "It is the least my wife and I can do for you, my lad," he said, his voice breaking with compassion.

Zafer continued to look after me as we made our way back to the docks. I noticed that two of the members of our crew were now working on this new ship. I was glad they had secured other positions.

"The skies are clear," the captain told us, "and the reports from arriving ships indicate we should expect smooth sailing. We will depart at daybreak tomorrow."

We arrived at the ship the next morning well before sunrise. It became obvious Zafer was not used to being on a ship he was not navigating. I watched him study how this crew conducted themselves as they cast off from the dock and made their way out into the open sea.

Apparently, the captain observed his behavior as well. As the two spoke throughout the day, the captain offered Zafer wise counsel.

"You will soon return to the helm, Zafer; but for now, allow this calm sea to replace the strength she took from you just days ago. Allow her gentle rocking to soothe the great pain she has inflicted upon you."

On our fifth day at sea, we made out the distant coastland of Cyprus. I suddenly realized we would be the ones conveying the devastating news to the families of the deceased. My grandparents had lost a son, just as I had lost a father. And the other families had also lost husbands, fathers, sons, brothers, and uncles. My heart broke at the thought of the pain we would be inflicting.

The captain deftly maneuvered his ship alongside the dock later that afternoon. I scanned the faces to see if I could locate my grandfather in the midst of the bustling activity. Though he had no reason to suspect I was aboard this ship, I thought he might have business in the harbor.

And I was correct. I spotted him speaking with a group of men on the dock. After we thanked the captain of this vessel for his kindness and hospitality, Zafer, the cook, and I hastily made our way down the gangplank toward my grandfather.

We were within a few feet of him when my grandfather spotted us. He looked both shocked and confused when he saw me. His eyes swept across the crowd in search of his son—then he turned his gaze pensively back toward me.

"John Mark, where is your father?" he asked, trying to steady his voice. "And Zafer, why are you men back here in Paphos so soon?"

"I regret to inform you, sir," Zafer began with some difficulty, "that your son, Captain Artemis, and two other crew members perished in a storm off the coast of Crete about a week ago. The ship and our cargo were lost as well. We are the only survivors."

My grandfather looked horror-struck as Zafer explained what had happened. His eyes welled with tears, and he reached out to pull me into his arms. Crushed against his heaving chest, I felt his grip around me tighten as he sobbed. Grandfather's sorrow spilled into mine, and the feelings I had repressed for the past week were unleashed.

Activity on the dock came to a standstill as everyone stopped to show their respect. Acquaintances of Zafer and the cook approached them to convey their condolences. Men who made their living by the sea knew that lurking behind its beauty was the real threat of death. They shared a common bond, and when one grieved, they all grieved.

Eventually my grandfather was able to express his condolences to Zafer and the cook. He also thanked Zafer for watching over me and bringing me back safely. He assured both men of his support when it came time for them to seek employment.

"In the meantime," he told them, "come by and see me in a few days, and I will provide you with money to help make up for the wages you have lost."

Zafer and the cook thanked my grandfather profusely for his compassion and concern. They then left to find their family members and those of the men who would not be returning. My grandfather and I slowly made our way home to repeat the exchange with my unsuspecting grandmother.

8

BACK HOME TO JERUSALEM

~

*L*ike most people in Cyprus, residents of Paphos worshiped the Greek goddess Aphrodite. In fact, the city had built a large temple in her honor. Pilgrims from throughout the Roman Empire journeyed to the city to pay homage to her.

However, my grandparents worshiped with the much smaller religious community of Jews. Though not devout in their beliefs, my grandparents felt the God of the Jews was much more trustworthy than a promiscuous goddess.

Nevertheless, the two religious beliefs did share one thing in common: neither believed there was life after death. So, my father's passing left my grandparents with a lack of hope, and they grieved without comfort.

In accordance with Jewish custom, my grandparents and their household immediately entered into a seven-day period of mourning. Their Jewish friends faithfully surrounded them during that time, but the days weighed heavily on us all.

My father attempted to tell my grandparents about Jesus before our departure for Sicily, but they had been unreceptive. Though I was young and a new believer in Jesus, I was reassured by what I had heard Him teach several times at the Temple: *"God gave His one and only Son, so that everyone who believes in Him will not perish but have eternal life."*[1]

I was confident I would see my father again. I didn't quite know how or when—and I missed him terribly—but I knew we would one day be reunited before Jesus. I tried to share that hope with my grandparents, but they ignored my words and considered them to be the foolish wishes of a grieving child. Though they did not openly refute my belief, they simply refused to accept it.

I waited for the seven days of mourning to pass before I made my wishes known that I needed to return home to my mother. On the eighth day, when I was alone with my grandfather, I raised the topic.

"Papa, I must go home to Jerusalem," I said. "Mother must be told about Father, and I need to take up my position as the man of our family. She will need me now, more than ever."

"Yes, you must return," Papa replied, "but I will go with you. You and your mother will need to move here to Paphos to be with family. I will assist your mother in settling your father's business affairs and making the necessary arrangements to close out your household."

"Move back to Paphos?" I responded in surprise. "But Jerusalem is our home. I do not believe Mother will want to move to Paphos."

"That is one of the reasons why I must come with you," my grandfather said. "I will help her understand why this is the only choice for the two of you."

As far as Papa was concerned the matter was settled, and I knew it was not my place to debate the issue with him. I also knew my mother would be more than capable of doing so herself once she got over the initial shock of our news.

Two days later, my grandfather and I set sail on a merchant ship headed for the port city of Joppa. Though I was a little nervous to be on a boat again, the weather was clear, the seas were calm, and the sailing was smooth. We arrived at our destination in three days.

Once we were ashore, Papa arranged with one of the traders my father did business with to borrow two of his donkeys. When the man learned of my father's fate, he was more than willing to help us. It took us a day and a half to reach Jerusalem astride the mules.

When we arrived at my home, a servant named Martha was the first to spot me. My grandfather had his back toward us as he tended the donkeys and she mistook him for my father.

"Your mother will be so glad to hear the two of you have returned!" Martha exclaimed. "We were not expecting you for another couple of weeks. She will be beside herself with joy!"

She immediately ran off to find my mother, giving me no opportunity to correct her misunderstanding. Within moments, Mother raced from the house to embrace me.

"I don't know how the two of you finished your business so quickly, but I thank God for your swift return!" she told us excitedly. She hugged me, then turned to hug the man she thought was my father.

But she stopped short when she realized she was looking into the eyes of her father-in-law.

"Papa, what are you doing here?" she cried out. "I had no idea you would be returning with Damaris and John Mark. It is a wonderful surprise!"

Mother was looking around for my father when she noticed there were only two donkeys tied to the rail.

"Where is Damaris?" she anxiously asked my grandfather. "Was he not traveling with you?"

But my grandfather's and my expressions revealed the answer she had already begun to fear. Before we could reply, my mother fell to her knees and began to wail. "Where is my husband?" she sobbed.

I knelt beside her and placed my arm around her. "He was lost at sea, Mother," I said softly. "Our ship was destroyed by a terrible storm off the coast of Crete. Father and two other men were swept out to sea by the pounding waves. The captain tried to save them, but he, too, became a victim of the storm.

"I wanted to swim after Father, but the seas were just too fierce. I would have drowned as well, but the helmsman kept me afloat through the night and helped me make it to shore the next day."

Mother looked into my eyes and sobbed, "You mean I could have lost you both? But God in His gracious providence saved you to spare me that pain!"

She and I remained on our knees embracing for quite a while. Periodically she would ask a question about the accident. Gradually the entire story was told, including how I had made it back to Paphos and was reunited with my grandparents.

"I am so sorry, John Mark," she said tenderly. "No boy should ever have to suffer what you did. Your father and I discussed whether it was safe for you to make the trip, and we both agreed that it was. But we were wrong … and I am sorry."

Gratefully, God gave me wisdom beyond my years when I replied.

"Mother, you have nothing to be sorry about. It was a storm, and no one could have prevented it. Everyone on board did the best they could to keep us all safe. I will never understand why Father died and I lived, but I have to trust that God has a purpose in all of this. And one day, just like Jesus promised, we will see one another again!"

Papa had been quietly standing by as my mother and I spoke; out of the corner of my eye I noticed a tear trickle down his cheek. Although I didn't realize it at the time, my grandfather had witnessed the comforting power of God's Spirit in our lives. It was the first expression of comfort and hope he had experienced concerning my father's death.

In the years to come, I learned that the Spirit of God used that exchange between my mother and me to lead my grandfather to Jesus. It was far more powerful than any word of argument my father or I could have ever chosen to offer up.

~

9

A FUTURE AND A HOPE

apa waited three days to tell my mother of his plans to take us back to Paphos.

"The business here in Jerusalem is doing well," my mother told my grandfather. "There is no reason for John Mark and me to return to Paphos."

"There is every reason for you to return," Papa replied. "Who will oversee this side of the business now that Damaris is gone? And without a functioning business, what will you and your son live on? John Mark is too young, and I cannot stay here. I need to remain in Paphos to keep our relationships with our trading partners strong."

"I will run the business!" my mother countered. "You know Damaris did not have a mind for business. He was a good husband and father, and he was a hard worker whom everyone loved. I know you are aware that we made all decisions together. Likewise, you know the idea to begin this salt trade originated with me. I'm the one who recognized the opportunity and devised the plan. I convinced you that it would work, then you presented it to Damaris as if it were your idea."

Up to this point, neither my mother nor my grandfather seemed concerned about my being in the room. But after that last remark, Papa glanced over at me.

"Perhaps John Mark should leave us while we continue this conversation," he said.

"No," my mother adamantly replied. "This is his home and his future we are discussing. He has a right to be here as we make decisions that will affect the rest of his life."

Papa sighed as he continued, "Yes, I know the role you have played in all of this. Your father taught you well. But Damaris was the one people saw as the proprietor of this business. I doubt the leaders of the Temple in Jerusalem or the fisheries in Galilee would have entered into a business relationship with a woman. We must be realistic. Your customers and suppliers are not prepared to do business with a woman!"

"One day, I pray that will no longer be true," my mother replied. "But I agree that is currently the case. However, I may have a solution. My nephew Joseph has begun to work with us. He is becoming a recognized and respected member of our community. If Joseph is the one who represents our business, we should have no issues with our customers and suppliers. He will need to withdraw from his studies under Rabbi Gamaliel, but he has already said that he would.

"It makes sense that, in light of Damaris's death, you would entrust the day-to-day running of the business to Joseph. That way, I can continue my role, and we will continue benefiting from the success of my efforts. I will live in Jerusalem as a wealthy widow enjoying the prosperous lifestyle provided by her husband's shrewd business skills. John Mark can continue his schooling, and you can continue to enjoy your portion of the profits this business produces."

Though I knew my mother would prevail in this conversation, even I had underestimated her abilities! The look on Papa's face told me we would not be moving to Paphos. A few days later, my grandfather set off on his journey back home.

Mother's predictions regarding the fate of the business were correct. Joseph successfully took on the public mantle of leadership and was comfortable taking direction from my mother. The increase in trade my father had anticipated did materialize and exceeded even my mother's expectations.

I continued to excel in my studies and had a list of questions for Jesus the next time I saw Him. That occurred when He returned to Jerusalem for Passover. I was delighted when He and some of His disciples stayed with Mother and me. His entourage had now swelled to almost forty people.

But all my questions disappeared the moment Jesus entered our home. The first thing He did was kneel beside me so He could look me in the eye and put His arm around me.

"John Mark," He began, "I have asked the Father to send His Spirit to comfort you and your mother. Not long ago, my mother and I experienced the death of my earthly father. I know the pain death causes, but I also know that in the world to come, my earthly father and your father will have eternal life because they believed in Me. That is why My Heavenly Father sent Me.[1]

"And John Mark, be ever mindful that I know the plans the Father has for you. They are plans for good and not for disaster, to give you a future and a hope."[2]

Words cannot describe what Jesus's assurances meant to a grieving ten-year-old boy. I was in awe when He told me He prayed for me—and that He knew the plans for my life!

Another memorable event during that visit was meeting a fisherman named Simon, whom Jesus had apparently renamed Peter. I was small for my age, so Peter looked like a giant. He had the biggest hands I had ever seen and a ruddy complexion that comes from spending a lifetime on the sea.

It was obvious that the other disciples looked to him for leadership. Most often, when Jesus asked His disciples a question, Peter was the first to answer. I tended to be somewhat timid and reserved, so I admired his boldness.

And you could always tell when Peter was in a room. He had a booming voice, and his laugh was unmistakable. As I got to know the disciples better, I discovered that I am a lot like Peter's brother, Andrew—the disciple who first introduced our family to Jesus. It's difficult to describe, but Peter and I immediately developed a bond that I believe will last a lifetime.

Not long after Jesus and His disciples left, my cousin Joseph approached my mother as we were eating our evening meal.

"Mary, I believe I am supposed to begin traveling with Jesus when He returns for Passover next spring. But in the meantime, I will need to prepare someone to step into my role in the business."

"I can fill that role, Mother!" I quickly declared.

"I have no doubt you would do an excellent job, John Mark, but I fear you are still too young," Mother gently replied. "I do not believe our customers or suppliers would show an eleven-year-old boy the respect that position requires. One day you will, my son, but it is still too early."

"I have been considering my cousin Mnason," Joseph suggested. "He has completed his studies under Rabbi Gamaliel, and his father encouraged him to seek an opportunity apart from his family's business. His father believes he will gain more valuable experience if he is not the owner's son.

"Mnason has a good head for business, he is trustworthy, and a quick learner. I believe I could train him to take over my role by next spring."

"I agree he has the maturity and business skills," Mother replied, "but he is not a follower of Jesus. And I prefer that whoever assumes this position is like-minded in their beliefs."

"I concur," Joseph responded, "but Mnason is seeking the truth. And I fully believe that one day he will embrace our Lord!"

Two weeks later, Mnason became Joseph's understudy. And when the following Passover celebration took place, Joseph set out with Jesus as one of His followers.

Whenever their entourage returned to Jerusalem, Joseph stayed with us while the others lodged elsewhere. However, Mother and I always went to the Temple to listen to Jesus teach anytime He was there.

I will never forget the day my mother and I observed Jesus enter the city riding a donkey's colt. It was exciting to watch the crowd as they welcomed Him. Many spread their coats on the road ahead of Him, while others laid leafy branches in His path. All around Him people were shouting:

"Praise God!
Bless the One who comes in the name of the Lord!
Bless the coming Kingdom of our ancestor David!
Praise God in highest heaven!" [3]

10

THE WEEK OF PASSOVER

~

*I*f looks could kill, Jesus would have been dead long before His celebratory entry into the city ended.

The religious leaders' animosity toward Him only intensified as Passover approached. Even as Jesus walked through the Temple that day, Pharisees peered at Him from the corners of the courtyard like vultures awaiting their prey.

My mother and I were surprised, though, when Jesus left the Temple without speaking to the huge crowd assembled.

"The people were expecting Jesus to declare Himself to be the Messiah," my mother told me. "They were ready to crown Him king and declare their loyalty. Instead, He quietly exited the city. No one knows what to make of that. I must confess, I don't know what to make of it either."

A hush fell over Jerusalem that night. I'm not sure if it was because people were disappointed or because they were anticipating what might happen the next day. Regardless, I slept very little that night. I was up before dawn and headed out for the Temple before my mother had awakened.

I was shocked when I saw money changers and merchants had set up their stalls inside the Temple. They hadn't been there the day before. As a matter of fact, they hadn't been there since Jesus drove them out three years earlier.

At first, it was a whisper coming from those near the entry. But soon it rose to a clamor: "Jesus is coming. He's here!"

I thought He would be stunned to see merchants assembled in the Temple —but He was not. With eyes like flint, He immediately knocked over their tables and stalls saying, *"The Scriptures declare, 'My Temple will be called a place of prayer for all nations,' but you have turned it into a den of thieves!"* [1]

The merchants obviously were expecting Jesus's reaction. Rather than resist Him, they simply picked up the remains of their trade and left. As I looked around, I noticed the Pharisees covertly watching Jesus with contempt. But they didn't say or do anything; instead, it was as if they were observing carefully orchestrated events unfold.

Jesus taught for the rest of the day in the Court of the Women. He frequently chose that place because no one could be excluded from hearing Him. The religious leaders watched as those Jesus healed and even the children began to shout, *"Praise God for the Son of David!"* [2]

The leaders became more and more indignant. *"Do You hear what these children are saying?"* [3] they asked Jesus.

"Yes," He replied. *"Haven't you ever read the Scriptures? For they say, 'You have taught children and infants to give You praise.'"* [4]

Jesus continued to teach and heal people throughout the day. As the afternoon drew to an end, He announced to His disciples that it was time to go. The religious leaders had stared at Him the entire time but never did anything. Perhaps they knew they had no power over Jesus.

The following day was the same: He taught, and He healed. The religious leaders periodically asked Jesus questions trying to catch Him in an error or a contradiction of the Law of Moses. But their efforts failed and simply highlighted their lack of knowledge concerning the Scriptures. Eventually they stopped in order to save themselves further embarrassment.

As Jesus and His disciples were leaving, Joseph came over to tell my mother and me they would not be returning to Bethany that night. Rather, Jesus and His apostles would spend the night on the Mount of Olives. Joseph asked if he could lodge with us.

"Of course!" Mother replied smiling.

"Actually, Jesus will not be returning to the Temple for the next two days," Joseph continued. "He has decided to spend time away from the crowds with His Heavenly Father before the dawning of the Festival of Unleavened Bread."

On Wednesday, I enjoyed catching up with Joseph, but I missed hearing more of Jesus's teaching. I reflected on all I had learned from Him, but my soul hungered for more. *Why had Jesus not yet declared Himself to be the Messiah? What was He waiting for? Surely it would happen this week here in Jerusalem! He would assume the throne of David, and everything would be set right.*

The next day I decided to wait by the Sheep Gate, which is the one Jesus and His disciples most often used. (Jesus had entered the city through the Eastern Gate, or King's Gate, the day He rode in on a donkey). I waited patiently in hopes of seeing Him or at least one of His disciples.

A little while later, I spotted Peter, John, and Shimon (the shepherd) entering through the gate.

"I have been waiting here all morning in the hopes I would see you," I excitedly told Peter. "I have missed being with you these past two days. Can I walk with you now?"

Peter smiled and put his arm around me. "Of course you can, my young friend."

"Where are you going?" I asked.

"We don't know," Peter replied somewhat sheepishly.

I looked at him with a quizzical expression. "Then how will you know when you get there?"

John abruptly interrupted us. "There's the man carrying the pitcher of water that Jesus told us about. We must follow him!"

I decided it wasn't the right time to ask more questions, so I simply enjoyed walking with them. The man ultimately led us to the shop of Yitzhak the weaver. I knew it well; my mother frequented his shop. But the man did not go into the shop. Instead, he led us to an upper room above the shop.

"Your master has provided just as Jesus told us he would," Peter said to the servant. "Please convey the Lord's thanks."

Shimon left the room but soon returned with several women who would prepare the Seder meal, a ceremonial feast that commemorates the Jews' exodus from Egypt.

"So, is this where you all will observe the Passover meal?" I asked.

"Yes, it is," Peter replied. "Would you and your mother like to join us?"

"I would love to! But Mother is already busily preparing for *our* Seder, which will include our entire household. Will Jesus return to the Temple tomorrow? If so, I will see you there."

"Jesus has not yet told us what He plans to do tomorrow," Peter said. "Watch for us at the gate, just as you did this morning."

I hurried home to help my mother. At sunset, we celebrated the Seder. Since I was now of age, Mother said I would lead the reading in our home this year. It was a great honor, but it was at times like these that I particularly missed my father.

That evening as I lay in bed, my mind was filled with thoughts. *What if Jesus and the disciples do not return through the Sheep Gate tomorrow? Joseph will not know where to find them, and neither will I!* So I decided to slip out of the house and go back to Yitzhak's shop. Perhaps I could ask Jesus directly.

I arrived in time to see Jesus and His disciples heading toward the Mount of Olives. I did not want to intrude, so I followed them at a distance. I would wait for an appropriate time to ask Jesus my question.

When we arrived at the mount, Jesus told all but three of the disciples to wait there and pray for Him. He took Peter, James, and John farther up the mount and instructed them to do the same. Then Jesus walked a short distance away and knelt in prayer.

I realized this was not the time to interrupt them, so I found a place in the bushes and waited. I would just follow them in the morning. Hopefully, Mother would understand why I left home without telling her and stayed out all night. After all, I was with Jesus. What could possibly happen with Him around?

Soon, I fell into a deep sleep.

∼

11

A PLACE CALLED GOLGOTHA

~

"*J*ohn Mark, can you hear me?"

My head throbbed as I slowly opened my eyes. Gradually, my cousin Joseph came into focus. I winced in pain as I tried to sit up.

"What happened?"

"One of the soldiers leading Jesus from the Antonia Fortress to the cross struck you with his club," Joseph replied. "You've been lying here unconscious in this ditch for quite some time. I ran after you when you left home this morning and arrived in time to see the soldier hit you. Do you remember anything?"

"Yes," I answered haltingly. "It's somewhat jumbled in my brain. The soldiers and priests arrested Jesus on the Mount of Olives. Everyone abandoned Him.

"I ran home to tell Mother, and she sent word to Joseph the Pharisee. He told us what was happening. I ran to the fortress to see for myself what they were doing to Jesus.

"I cried out when I saw His battered body and that is when the soldier hit me. Do you know where they are taking Jesus?"

"To Golgotha to be crucified," Joseph replied.

"What can we do?"

"The only thing any of us can do now—and the only thing Jesus would want us to do—is pray," Joseph answered.

"But we must go there!" I insisted. "We must be with Him."

"You are in no condition to go anywhere right now," Joseph responded sternly. "I will take you home so your mother can care for you, and then I will join the others at Golgotha."

As I shakily stood to my feet, I realized he was right. Joseph half carried me to my home, which we were grateful wasn't far away.

My mother met us at the door; she looked horrified as she studied the injury to my head. Joseph quickly explained what had taken place and then left to join the others at the foot of Jesus's cross. Mother ushered me to bed.

"But Mother, we must go to the place where they are crucifying Jesus!" I pleaded. "Surely with your position in the community you can convince someone to stop what is happening!"

"There is nothing any of us can do, John Mark," my mother replied sadly. "Pilate has signed his death warrant. Only the Heavenly Father or Caesar can stop it at this point. But the former doesn't seem so inclined, and the latter wouldn't make the effort even if he were here. I know the Heavenly Father must have a purpose in this, but I cannot imagine His pain in seeing what they are doing to His Son.

"All we can do is pray that what is to happen will occur quickly and according to the Father's will," she continued. "In the meantime, you must stay in bed."

As hard as it was to accept what my mother was saying, I knew she was speaking the truth. So I lay there and wept . . . and prayed.

It was midday when the skies turned dark. It seemed even the Father could not bear to see what was happening to His Son. Late in the afternoon, a messenger arrived to tell us Jesus was dead. The Pharisees Joseph and Nicodemus were making arrangements to bury Jesus's body in a tomb.

With sunset rapidly approaching, everyone else returned to their lodgings for the beginning of Sabbath. Nothing more could be done at this point.

My mother and I mourned as deeply for the death of Jesus as we had for the death of my father. This Sabbath day felt like none other: the Messiah was dead, and all our hopes were gone. He had promised me I would see my father again. *But how could that happen now that He was dead and buried?* I stayed in bed that day—less because my body hurt and more because I felt like there was nothing to live for.

The sun rose on Sunday just like any other day. But as soon as I awoke I remembered this wasn't like the days that had come before it. Our entire household was blanketed by grief and despair. So it surprised me when I heard a commotion later in the day. I was too curious to stay in bed, so I carefully made my way to the front entry to investigate.

My cousin Joseph was animatedly speaking to my mother.

"When the women arrived at the tomb this morning to anoint His body, the large stone at the entry had been rolled back. When they entered the tomb, they saw a young man sitting on the right side, dressed in a white robe. He said to them, 'Do not be surprised. You are looking for Jesus, the Nazarene, who was crucified. He isn't here! He has been raised from the dead! Look this is where they laid His body.'" [1]

I could not believe my ears! Joseph continued, "Jesus later appeared to Mary Magdalene and instructed her to tell His followers to gather tonight in the room above Yitzhak's shop."

Mother reached out to embrace me as she joyfully declared to Joseph, "We will be there!"

Nothing could have prepared us for Jesus's arrival that night in the upper room. Mother and I were captivated as those to whom He had appeared that day excitedly shared their encounter. Then suddenly … He appeared in our midst!

Almost everyone shrunk back in fear before Jesus said, *"Peace be with you!"* [2] As realization slowly dawned on us, we began to rejoice and praise God that Jesus was alive! After He spoke with us for a while, Jesus departed as quickly as He had arrived. Still, He appeared to the apostles twice more and to another 500 people at multiple times over the next several weeks.

Almost six weeks passed from that night in the upper room until my mother, my cousin Joseph, and I saw Him again. We were assembled with others on the Mount of Olives.

"Go into all the world and preach the Good News to everyone, everywhere. Anyone who believes and is baptized will be saved,"[3] Jesus declared to all of us.

And with that, He ascended into the sky and disappeared into a cloud. Our hearts were saddened to see Him go—but this time we knew beyond a shadow of a doubt we would see Him again.

12

A MIGHTY WINDSTORM

~

For the next ten days, my mother, cousin Joseph, household servants, and I gathered with the apostles and other followers to pray, just as Jesus had instructed. We waited for God to send the Helper Jesus had promised. The Helper would be His Holy Spirit through whom we would receive power. No one quite knew what that meant, we simply knew to obey, pray, and wait.

As we gathered on the tenth day, there was a sound from heaven like the roaring of a mighty windstorm. Suddenly, what looked like flames or tongues of fire appeared and settled upon each individual. We each began to speak in a language that was foreign to us.

We discovered these were signs that the Holy Spirit had come to dwell within us. He gave each of us different gifts, just as He had given us the ability to speak different languages.

When people on the street heard the sounds coming from our room, they came running to see what was happening. They were bewildered to hear

their own languages being spoken by those they considered to be unedu-
cated men. Some in the crowd even went so far as to say, *"They're drunk,
that's all!"*[1]

It was Peter who boldly stepped forward in front of the other apostles and
shouted to the crowd, *"Listen carefully, all of you, fellow Jews and residents of
Jerusalem! Make no mistake about this. Some of you are saying these people are
drunk. It isn't true! It's much too early for that. No, what you see this morning
was predicted centuries ago by the prophet Joel."*[2]

Peter went on to remind the crowd of those words recorded by the
prophet, saying:

> *"'In the last days,' God says, 'I will pour out My Spirit upon all people.*
> *Your sons and daughters will prophesy.*
> *Your young men will see visions,*
> *and your old men will dream dreams.*
> *In those days I will pour out My Spirit*
> *even on My servants—men and women alike—*
> *and they will prophesy.*
> *And I will cause wonders in the heavens above*
> *and signs on the earth below—*
> *blood and fire and clouds of smoke.*
> *The sun will become dark, and the moon will turn blood red*
> *before that great and glorious day of the Lord arrives.*
> *But everyone who calls on the name of the Lord will be saved.'"*[3]

Peter then continued to preach about Jesus with an eloquence and
anointing he had never previously demonstrated. It was obvious that the
Holy Spirit was speaking through him. As the day progressed, each of the
apostles spoke with that same anointing.

Before the day was over about 3,000 professed their faith in Jesus and were
baptized in the mikveh pools surrounding the Temple. They joined us in

devoting themselves to the apostles' teaching and fellowship, as well as sharing in the Lord's Supper and in prayer.

The religious leaders watched from the fringes with the same contempt they had shown for Jesus. They had mistakenly believed that by killing Jesus they would put an end to the threat His popularity posed to their position and power. They had even attempted to discredit the reports of His resurrection and accused His followers of abducting and hiding His body.

But now, their feeble attempts to cover the truth were having no effect. More and more people were being added to the church every day—even from the ranks of the religious leaders. Members of the Sanhedrin advised their leaders to take action, but none of them knew what action to take. Pontius Pilate had made it abundantly clear that he would not endorse any additional unwarranted crucifixions.

The apostles Peter and John were soon arrested for teaching about Jesus. They were brought before the high council and warned not to speak in His name again. Later that night, as followers gathered in my mother's home, Peter and John told us what they had said to the Sanhedrin: *"Do you think God wants us to obey you rather than Him? We cannot stop telling about the wonderful things we have seen and heard."* [4]

That night, we all lifted our voices in prayer, saying, *"O Lord, hear the threats of those who are united against You, and give us, Your servants, great boldness in preaching Your word. Stretch out Your hand with healing power; may miraculous signs and wonders be done through the name of Your holy servant Jesus."* [5]

When we finished, the building shook, and we were all filled with the Holy Spirit. The Heavenly Father continued to draw us together in one heart and one mind. We even began to view our personal possessions differently.

Mother and Joseph discussed the profits from the family business. God had continued to prosper the salt trade, and they both knew it was so those profits could help provide for the needs of the growing church.

"I will let the apostles know that each month's surplus from our business will now be given as an offering to provide for those who have need," my mother said.

"And I will sell the field I have been holding onto and give the proceeds to the church," added my cousin. "I always thought God had given it to me to plant, but now I know He entrusted it to me to give away."

Joseph made a substantial profit when he sold the land he had purchased ten years earlier. As he presented the proceeds to the apostles, Peter told him, "Joseph, you are a great encouragement to all of us—not only through this gift, but also through the many ways you serve and meet the needs of others. From now on we're going to call you 'Barnabas,' which means 'son of encouragement.'"

Although Barnabas wanted to keep the gift anonymous, news quickly spread among believers. But as Peter told him, "Who knows, Barnabas, the Lord may use your selfless act to encourage others He is prompting to take a similar step of obedience."

Two new believers meeting with us were an older couple named Ananias and Sapphira. Like so many others, they had believed and been baptized on the day of Pentecost. About a week after Barnabas had presented his proceeds, the husband and wife came forward to present a gift to the apostles. However, they did so very publicly so everyone could hear.

"Here are all the proceeds from the sale of some of our land. Use these funds to help those in need," Ananias announced to Peter. Afterward, he stood waiting for Peter to acknowledge his and his wife's generosity and selflessness.

Instead, Peter said, *"Ananias, why have you let Satan fill your heart? You lied to the Holy Spirit, and you kept some of the money for yourself. The property was yours to sell or not sell, as you wished. And after selling it, the money was also yours to give away. How could you do a thing like this? You weren't lying to us, but to God!"*[6]

When Peter finished, Ananias immediately died. Everyone gathered in our home was terrified. Several young men got up, wrapped Ananias's body in a sheet, and took him out and buried him.

Sapphira arrived about three hours later, unaware of what had happened to her husband. Peter asked her, *"Was this the price you and your husband received for your land?"*[7]

"Yes," she replied, *"that was the price."*[8]

Peter shook his head and said, *"How could the two of you even think of conspiring to test the Spirit of the Lord like this? The young men who buried your husband are just outside the door, and they will carry you out, too."*[9]

Instantly, she fell to the floor dead. When the young men returned to the room and saw Sapphira, they carried her body outside and buried her beside her husband.

A great fear of God gripped the entire church!

∼

13

GOD HAS COUNTED US WORTHY

～

"*G*od has counted us worthy to suffer dishonor for the name of Jesus!*"*[1] Peter declared several nights later to the followers gathered in our home.

He began to share the events that had taken place. The previous day, the twelve apostles had been arrested at Solomon's Colonnade in the Temple, by order of Caiaphas and the high council, and placed in jail. But an angel of the Lord came in the night, opened the gates of the jail, and freed the twelve.

"*Go to the Temple and give the people this message of life!*"[2] the angel commanded them.

The apostles had obediently entered the Temple at daybreak and began to teach. Several hours passed before the captain of the guard, together with the same temple guards who had arrested them before, came and directed the apostles to follow them. Apparently they had caused quite a stir that morning when it was discovered they were not in jail. Yet, that paled in comparison to the high council's amazement when they learned the apostles had been teaching right under their noses while everyone was searching for them!

"We gave you strict orders never again to teach in Jesus's name!" Caiaphas declared as they stood before him. *"Instead, you have filled all Jerusalem with your teaching about Him, and you want to make us responsible for His death!"*[(3)]

"But we told the council," Peter proclaimed, *"'we must obey God rather than any human authority. The God of our ancestors raised Jesus from the dead after you killed Him by hanging Him on a cross. Then God put Him in the place of honor at His right hand as Prince and Savior. He did this so the people of Israel would repent of their sins and be forgiven. We are witnesses of these things and so is the Holy Spirit, who is given by God to those who obey Him.'*[(4)]

"Several members of the council ruled that we should be killed. So the guards took us to another room until our fate was decided. To our surprise, rather than a verdict of death, the guards were instructed to flog us before returning us to the high council.

"'You must never again speak in the name of Jesus!' the high priest declared before directing the guards to usher us out of the Temple. But he never gave us the opportunity to remind him that we would only obey God. Instead, we left the chamber praising God for His goodness and faithfulness, for allowing us to share in the suffering of our Lord."

The size of our fellowship rapidly increased as the years passed. This influx of new believers brought with it two unexpected challenges. First, there were rumblings of discontent from within the church. Those who spoke Greek complained about those who spoke Hebrew, saying their widows were being discriminated against in the daily distribution of food.

The apostles wisely prompted the church to choose seven men who were respected, insightful, and filled with the Holy Spirit. They were to serve as deacons to oversee the food distribution and other business affairs of the body of believers.

But the second challenge was not quite so easily addressed. It was the persecution of the church. Caiaphas and the high council realized their sphere of influence and power were waning as more and more people became followers. To stem the tide, the religious leaders turned to the weapons in their arsenal that had always served them well—intimidation and threats of physical harm.

However, after the crucifixion of Jesus, Pontius Pilate and the Roman prefects who followed him warned Caiaphas and the high council they would not be drawn into any more of the Jews' religious squabbles. Roman leadership would no longer permit the crucifixion of anyone who had not broken Roman law. That removed one of the religious leaders' threats as they tried to prevent the mass exodus from Jewish orthodoxy.

So they decided to use death by stoning. It would appear to be an impromptu attack by a vengeful mob rather than a calculated execution.

Roman leaders had also informed the high priest that Jesus's apostles were not to be harmed. As word spread about the miracles the apostles were performing—combined with the increasing number of believers—the Romans were afraid any injury to the twelve could spark a rebellion.

One of the seven men chosen as a deacon was the first victim to be stoned. We all considered Stephanos to be a man full of God's grace and power. His command of the Scriptures, together with the amazing miracles God was performing through him, were bringing much notoriety.

But one day, several men from the Synagogue of Freed Slaves started an argument with Stephanos. They falsely accused him of blasphemy, and he was brought before the high council. The Holy Spirit prompted Stephanos to speak boldly before the council, concluding with these words:

"You stubborn people! You are heathen at heart and deaf to the truth. Must you forever resist the Holy Spirit? That's what your ancestors did, and so do you! Name one prophet your ancestors didn't persecute! They even killed the ones who predicted the coming of the Righteous One—the Messiah whom you betrayed and murdered. You deliberately disobeyed God's law, even though you received it from the hands of angels."[5]

Stephanos's accusations infuriated the Jewish leaders, and they shook their fists at him in rage. But witnesses said Stephanos gazed steadily up into heaven and saw the glory of God. He proclaimed, *"Look, I see the heavens opened and the Son of Man standing in the place of honor at God's right hand."*[6]

The religious leaders put their hands over their ears and shouted at a group of men to drag Stephanos out of the city and stone him.

I watched from a distance as the men hurled stones at him that day. In some respects, it was more evil than what I had witnessed when Jesus was led to Golgotha.

As he was pelted with stones, Stephanos prayed, *"Lord Jesus, receive my spirit."*[7] Then he fell to his knees and cried out, *"Lord, don't charge them with this sin!"*[8] And with that, he died.

One of the official witnesses who oversaw the killing was an ambitious young man named Saul—whose reputation as a zealous persecutor of the church grew from that day forward. His look of disdain troubled my spirit. I had never witnessed such hatred . . . and I feared this man greatly.

A tidal wave of persecution began that day, sweeping over the church in Jerusalem. Many believers—except the apostles—began to flee the city.

∾

14

A CHANGED MAN?

~

Several days after the stoning, Mnason mentioned a longtime friend named Saul who was lodging with him.

"Our friendship dates back to our years together as talmid in the school of Gamaliel," Mnason told my mother. "He recently returned to Jerusalem and sought me out. He is apparently carrying out duties on behalf of the high priest.

"I do not know the extent of his involvement, but be careful if you encounter him. He is an ambitious fellow, and he is working to get in the good graces of the high priest. Though I do not believe in Jesus, I also do not endorse what the religious leaders are doing. I do not want any harm to come to you or those who gather in your home to pray.

"So stay alert! I will warn you if Saul mentions anything that involves you or other followers. Until now, your family's standing in the community has been protecting you from persecution—but that may not always be the case."

Mother thanked Mnason for his candor. "However, we must be true to what we know the Master has called us to do," she added.

"It appears that the immediate threat to believers has subsided for the time being," Mnason told us a few days later. "Saul has been sent to the synagogues in Damascus with the high priest's authorization to arrest Jesus's followers there and bring them back to Jerusalem in chains. However, let your leaders know that Saul will return."

The stonings subsided in Jerusalem—at least temporarily. But we knew the persecutor and his companions would be back. However, as the weeks passed, there was no sign of him. The religious leaders even asked Mnason if he had any news concerning Saul.

We soon learned that his companions had returned from Damascus with news that Saul had been blinded by a brilliant light as they approached the city. They had left him to convalesce in the care of an acquaintance there. But since he was unable to carry out his mission, Saul had instructed them to return to Jerusalem.

Over the next several days, we heard varying reports of what had happened to Saul. One account said Jesus had appeared to him in the blinding light, and Saul was now a believer. Mnason, however, was confident that if that rumor were true, he would have received word. Having seen the evil of Saul's countenance when Stephanos was stoned, I was convinced this was just another ploy to keep the church off guard. The apostles taught that anyone was worthy of Jesus's forgiveness—but I was convinced that did not apply to Saul!

Three years passed, and the church continued to multiply beyond Jerusalem. Others had joined the apostles as leaders—most notably James, the half-brother of Jesus. They dedicated themselves to teaching us every-thing they had learned from the Lord during His time with them. That included what it meant to be followers of Jesus and how to walk in His steps.

When disagreements arose within the churches, the matter was referred to the leaders for a decision. It was not unusual for delegates from distant churches to seek their counsel. One day, an emissary arrived from the church in Damascus. Knowing that few would welcome him, he decided to first visit a trusted friend in the city.

The next morning, Mnason arrived at our home with joyful news.

"I have surrendered my life to Jesus!" he declared as he interrupted our morning meal.

Barnabas was the first to respond. He excitedly got up from his seat at the table and embraced Mnason as he said, "We rejoice in the decision you have made! You have no idea how long we have been praying for this day. Tell us how you came to that decision."

"Soon after sunset last night, there was a knock at my door. I was amazed to see my friend Saul."

Mother, Barnabas, and I exchanged looks of surprise.

"Saul and I stayed up all night as he explained how he had encountered Jesus on the road to Damascus and been left blind by the experience," Mnason continued. "A believer named Ananias bravely came to Saul's aid at the prompting of the Holy Spirit. God used Ananias to lay his hands on Saul for the restoration of his sight and to baptize him in his newfound faith.

"Saul went on to describe how the Spirit led him into the Arabian wilderness to be discipled by Jesus for these past three years. He spent time on Mount Hermon, in the cities of the Decapolis, as well as in Petra. Along the way, he experienced some of the same persecution that *he* had once inflicted.

"As Saul spoke, I saw a change in him that could not be contrived; neither could it have occurred without the supernatural work of a Holy God," Mnason told us. "By the time Saul finished, I knew I, too, needed to surrender my life to Jesus.

"Saul informed me I needed to be baptized and he would count it a privilege to be the one to do it. 'But,' he said, 'I would like to do so in the presence of the other believers here in Jerusalem. To do that, I need your help. Would you deliver a message that I have returned, and I would like to meet with the apostles?'"

Now that I was a young man of twenty-two and a more seasoned follower of Jesus, I felt qualified to offer my opinion.

"Mnason, I do not question your decision or the transformation in your life—but this sounds like Saul is setting a trap. He wants you to bring him into the presence of the apostles, but I fear he and his fellow persecutors will injure them . . . or worse!"

"Mark, I understand why you would think that. And it is definitely something the 'old Saul' would have done. But I have spent the night listening to this man, and I assure you he has changed," Mnason replied confidently. "The presence of the Spirit is evident in his life, just as it is in all of yours. I would never put any believer in danger, but I believe Saul's change of heart is genuine."

"Well," Barnabas thoughtfully replied, "we cannot risk putting the apostles in jeopardy; however, if the change in Saul's life is sincere, we must welcome our new brother in Christ with open arms. Mnason, I will accompany you back home to speak with Saul."

Later, Barnabas returned to our home to share his thoughts about the meeting.

"I listened attentively as Saul recounted what had occurred in his life during the past three years," he told us. "He said Jesus had given him the mandate to be the apostle to take His message to the Gentiles.

"'Though I am the least deserving of all God's people,' Saul had said, 'He has graciously given me the privilege of telling the Gentiles about the endless treasures available to them in Christ.'[1]

"As I listened, the Spirit of the Lord removed all my doubts," Barnabas continued. "I went to the apostles on Saul's behalf and advocated for them to meet with him. Though they trusted me, several were still skeptical. Finally, the apostles decided Saul would meet only with Peter and James, the half-brother of Jesus."

Barnabas went on to say that Peter and James had many questions for Saul, as he did for them. In addition to telling them about his encounter on the road to Damascus, Saul told them about the many believers he had met since then.

Simon Peter was particularly intrigued to hear about Saul's encounters in the Arabian wilderness with several people who had been touched by Jesus. They were now discipling new believers in the cities of the Decapolis—including the servant whose ear had been cut off in the Garden of Gethsemane. The message of Christ was spreading!

Though Peter and James—as well as my cousin Barnabas—now considered Saul a changed man, I still had my doubts. Though I hadn't yet spoken to him in person, it would take a whole lot more than words to change my opinion of the man who I had seen participate in the stoning of Stephanos!

~

15

THE GENTILES IN ANTIOCH

~

*S*aul remained in Jerusalem for two weeks—meeting with Peter, James, and Barnabas—as well as preaching throughout the city. I observed him on multiple occasions, including the nights he joined other followers in our home for prayer. Slowly, my opinion of him began to change. The reports of what he had seen and experienced the past three years bore witness to the power of God working in and through his life.

But not everyone was happy with the change that had occurred in Saul's life. The Hellenistic Jews, particularly those who had participated in the trial and death of Stephanos, vividly remembered that Saul had been one of them. They began to debate him, but Saul boldly witnessed to them just as Stephanos had. The high council became increasing incensed that Saul was now openly preaching the message of Jesus throughout the city.

Word soon spread that they were planning to murder him. Peter and James decided it was time for Saul to leave Jerusalem for his own safety. Saul believed Jesus had given him an assignment among the Gentiles, and he knew it must start in his hometown of Tarsus. A trusted source told us the Jews were watching for Saul along the road to Joppa, the port city from which they expected him to depart. Instead, we devised a plan for several men to accompany Saul to the port in Caesarea.

Saul told us he needed to do one thing before he left Jerusalem. He invited Mnason, Peter, James, Barnabas, my mother, and me to join him at one of the mikveh pools outside the temple. We watched with great joy as Saul baptized Mnason, who publicly declared his faith in Jesus the Messiah. Our family and Saul now shared a strong bond—the salvation of Mnason.

I offered to go with Barnabas and Mnason as they accompanied Saul to Caesarea, but Barnabas said I should stay in Jerusalem and keep a watchful eye over my mother. "Besides," he added, "I have little doubt we will see Saul again, and something tells me it will provide more opportunities for us to travel with him."

As the years rolled by, the Good News of Jesus traveled from Jerusalem to the Jews living in Phoenicia, Syria, Cyprus, Cyrene, and other faraway places. We knew my grandfather had carried it back to Paphos, and Saul had most certainly begun to spread the word in Tarsus.

But the message was not being preached only to the Jews; large numbers of Gentiles were now followers. That was the missive delivered from Antioch of Syria to the leaders of the church in Jerusalem: "The power of the Lord has come upon the Gentiles, and large numbers have believed."

"We must send someone to investigate this report," James declared one evening while he and several of the other leaders were gathered in our home. "Barnabas, would you go for us? You have the maturity to discern the validity of what is happening and the giftedness to teach these new believers and encourage them in their walk."

"How long do you want me to stay there?" Barnabas asked.

"As long as it takes," James replied. "If this report is genuine, you will need to stay and train leaders for the church."

"I will go," he responded, "but only if is satisfactory with Mary."

All eyes in the room turned to my mother.

"Barnabas," she said," you have faithfully honored the commitment you made to my late husband almost twenty years ago—as well as the commitment you made to me after his death. God blessed our business even while you were traveling with Jesus, and He will do so again as you go to Antioch. Besides, Mnason and John Mark have proven they can carry on the work here. I will not stand in your way."

"Then it is settled," Barnabas declared.

He took the next day to prepare for his three-week journey over land to Antioch. The city boasts a population of half a million people, which makes it the third-largest city in the Roman Empire, surpassed only by Rome and Alexandria. Because it is a busy port city and a center for luxury and culture, it attracts all kinds of people—including wealthy, retired Roman officials who spend their days conversing in the baths or gambling at the chariot races.

With Antioch's cosmopolitan population and its commercial and political power, its residents want for very little. It is also a wicked city filled with self-indulgent temptations, perhaps eclipsed only by Corinth. Though all the Syrian, Greek, and Roman deities are honored in the city, the principal shrine is dedicated to Daphne, whose worship includes immoral rituals.

Barnabas was overjoyed when he saw proof of God's favor in the lives of the believers and how the Good News was flourishing in the city. He immediately began encouraging and teaching them how to remain strong in their faith and true to the Lord.

But he quickly realized he needed more help, and the Lord impressed upon him to enlist Saul. It had been almost seven years since Barnabas had said farewell to Saul in Caesarea. He had no idea if Saul would still be in his hometown, but he sensed the Spirit of God directing him to make the eight-day journey there.

Barnabas sent a message to the leaders in Jerusalem confirming the accuracy of the initial reports and detailing his plan to find Saul and bring him back to Antioch. He set out the next day for the capital city of the province of Cilicia—the city of Tarsus.

"As I walked through Tarsus, I came upon a group of men and women gathered in the city square listening to a man whose voice I instantly recognized," Barnabas later shared with me. "'What are you doing here in Tarsus?' Saul asked me once he had finished teaching.

"As soon as I told him what the Spirit of God was doing among the Gentile believers in Antioch and my need for a co-laborer, he immediately agreed to return with me.

"Saul and I continued teaching the growing number of believers in Antioch for the next year. Toward the end of our time there, a group of prophets arrived from Jerusalem. Their spokesman was a man named Agabus. He stood up in one of our meetings, clearly empowered by the Spirit of God, and predicted a great famine would soon come upon the entire Roman world.

"Saul and I watched as the believers reacted to this news. They were not concerned for themselves; instead, they worried how they could help their persecuted brothers and sisters in Judea. Believing that to whom much has been given, much is required, they took up an offering and gave as generously as they could. They were well aware the Gospel had been given to them at a great cost—the shed blood of Jesus and the shed blood of the Jerusalem martyrs.

"They chose to send their gifts to Jerusalem through Saul and me. It also gave us a chance to tell the elders what the Spirit was doing among the Gentiles in Antioch. We set out for Jerusalem so we would arrive in time for the observance of Passover."

∼

16

A JOURNEY BEGINS

~

*B*arnabas and Saul were stunned when they arrived in Jerusalem. The church was in an uproar, and the political landscape had changed dramatically. Herod Antipas had fallen out of favor with Emperor Caligula and had been exiled to Spain. His nephew, Herod Agrippa, was now the new favored son of Rome.

The emperor had recalled the Roman prefect from Judea and had chosen to reunite the kingdom, which had been split after the death of Agrippa's grandfather, Herod the Great. Agrippa was appointed governor over the entire region of Judea, Samaria, Galilee, and Perea—and carried the title of king just as his grandfather had.

After Jesus's crucifixion, the Roman prefect had somewhat protected the apostles and elders of the Jerusalem church from retribution by the Jewish leaders. He had turned a blind eye to the stoning of Stephanos and other leaders but was clear that no one was to harm Peter, James, or the other apostles and elders. When the Roman prefect was recalled to Rome and Agrippa was appointed governor, that protection no longer existed.

King Agrippa knew he would curry favor with the Jewish rulers if he persecuted church leaders. One week before Barnabas and Saul entered Jerusalem, the apostle James— brother of John and son of Zebedee—was arrested.

James was targeted for several reasons. The high council knew Peter, John, and James comprised Jesus's innermost circle. John had a unique familial relationship with the Jewish leaders. He was the great-grand-nephew of Hillel the Elder and had briefly been a talmid of Rabbi Gamaliel. So the leaders had no interest in having him arrested. Peter was obviously the main spokesman, but they feared how people would react to his arrest. Though James was also related to Hillel, he had never walked in religious "aristocracy" circles; but rather, he had chosen the life of a simple fisherman.

Agrippa saw how pleased the Jewish leaders were when he had James killed with a sword. That emboldened him to have Peter arrested, too, which occurred the same day Barnabas and Saul arrived in Jerusalem. We learned that night about Agrippa's plan to make a public spectacle of Peter. Instead of simply putting him to death, Peter would be placed on trial to face the false charges against him.

Throughout the Passover, believers gathered in homes to pray for Peter's release. Barnabas and Saul joined the prayer gathering at our home, including the night before Peter was to be tried.

We had been praying for a while when one of our servants, Rhoda, entered the room and told us, *"Peter is standing at the door!"*[1]

"You're out of your mind!"[2] someone in the group replied.

But Rhoda insisted, so Mother and I followed her to the door. We were amazed to find Peter standing there! He motioned for us to be quiet as he explained that an angel had delivered him from his cell and led him out of prison. Before he left, he instructed us to send a message to James, the half-brother of Jesus, and the other elders explaining what had happened.

The next morning, word traveled quickly that Peter had disappeared. Agrippa's soldiers had searched for him throughout the night to no avail; the men guarding Peter were put to death. Agrippa was livid! He hastily left Jerusalem in humiliation for having been bested by a Galilean fisherman. But we believers knew it was a Galilean Carpenter who had defeated him!

As news of Peter's escape spread, so did the Good News. And there were many new believers as a result.

Unbeknownst to me, my mother approached Barnabas that morning about taking me back with him to Antioch. I was astonished when she told me what she had arranged.

"Mother, with both Barnabas *and* me gone, you will be left with only Mnason to assist you with the business. I feel I need to remain here and assume my role as father's heir to our family business."

"I understand, John Mark," my mother replied. "But what if God's plan for you is not to take over the business but rather to spread the Good News like Barnabas and Saul? Could it be that the passion you exhibited as a teenager to follow Jesus to the place of His betrayal—and even His crucifixion—was for this very purpose? Perhaps the young man who witnessed Stephanos's boldness in the face of persecution has been given that same boldness to make the Good News of Jesus known!

"What better way to know for sure than to spend time with Barnabas and Saul and allow the Holy Spirit to show you His plan for your life. Are you willing to do whatever He leads you to do?

"If the answer is for you to return and take over the business, you will have my full support. And if the answer is to do what Jesus said—to be His witness to the ends of the earth, then you will have my full support in that as well."

"Then I will go with them, Mother, and ask the Holy Spirit to give me guidance."

Two days later, an earthquake occurred in Antioch. Fearing the devastation we would find, Barnabas and Saul said we must go quickly.

It had been ten years since the last earthquake shook Antioch; Tiberius was emperor at the time. Shock waves from this recent quake had triggered a tsunami damaging harbors and ports as far away as Caesarea Maritima. But nothing could have prepared us for the destruction and death we saw when we arrived.

Witnesses told us the earthquake began with a loud roar and then the ground shook violently. Whole trees, along with people, were thrown into the air. Numerous residents were killed by falling debris from collapsing buildings. Aftershocks continued for several days, proving fatal for many still trapped in the ruins. Others died of starvation and dehydration before they could be rescued.

Two believers, Rufus and Aurelius, were killed by tumbling rubble while attempting to rescue others. Two others, Lucius and Manaen, were both injured in the wreckage. Simeon, an elder of the church, mobilized followers to assist in providing aid—food, shelter, and clothing—to those most severely impacted. The church responded quickly and selflessly.

By the time we arrived, nearly every church family was providing shelter to at least one displaced family. The community soon noticed it was the Christians, as believers were now being called, who were providing the most aid. Residents began asking why believers would selflessly help total strangers. As a result, many folks heard the Gospel and came to faith in Jesus.

Each day, Barnabas, Saul, and I rolled up our sleeves to help our brothers and sisters in ministering to the needs of the city. Then at night, Barnabas and Saul met with the growing number of new believers, discipling them in their newfound faith. I assisted however I could. Lucius and Manaen soon recovered from their injuries and also joined in the effort.

The physician Luke proved to be a remarkable instrument of God's mercy and grace as he labored tirelessly. Though he and his parents lived in Antioch, he had met Saul in Tarsus several years earlier, at which time he had become a believer.

Temporary facilities were set up to provide treatment for the injured. In most instances, those helping Luke were also believers. But Luke's care wasn't limited to physical needs; he also compassionately ministered to people's emotional needs.

I believe the earthquake was a turning point in the life of the church in Antioch. Believers transitioned from being silent followers of Jesus to becoming His hands and feet. They loved the people in their city with the love of Jesus—and the city saw it and responded.

As weeks turned into months and we were no longer in a crisis, I saw believers' relationships with Christ deepen and mature. They knew God was leading them to follow Him in even more meaningful ways.

Barnabas, Simeon, Lucius, Manaen, and Saul fasted and prayed as they sought God's guidance about next steps for the church. None of us could have imagined what or how monumental that step would be. God was about to use this church to impact the world.

One day as we gathered to worship, the Holy Spirit said to the leaders, *"Appoint Barnabas and Saul for the special work to which I have called them."*[3] Both knew Jesus had called and prepared them to take His message to the Gentiles. But the elders realized this was now also a call on the church. The Holy Spirit was directing them to send out Barnabas and Saul, and to support them with their prayers. Other members would be dispatched to assist them as needed. And the church was to support them all financially.

That evening, the leaders told the church what the Holy Spirit had said. God had called Barnabas and Saul and anointed them; the church was now to send them out. There were mixed emotions as believers processed everything. In the midst of the gathering, someone asked, "What about John Mark? Will he be going with them?"

I watched and listened as Barnabas and Saul discussed my fate. Should I stay in Antioch, return to Jerusalem, or go with them? Barnabas is the one who finally said, "Mary entrusted him into our care for us to nurture. It was never about the place. We are to nurture him wherever we go."

It became clear to Barnabas and Saul that the Holy Spirit was directing me to accompany them. I, however, wasn't so sure; but I deferred to how they believed God was leading. The elders—Simeon, Lucius, and Manaen—laid hands on us as the church prayed over us.

The next morning, the church sent the three of us on our way.

~

17

TRAVELING WITH SAUL AND BARNABAS

~

Saul and Barnabas felt the Lord leading them to first preach the Gospel across the island of Cyprus, so we departed Antioch on a ship bound for Salamis. It was smooth sailing on our two-day journey. We discovered that the ship's captain, Andreas, was friends with another captain named Andri, whom Saul had led to the Lord several years earlier.

Andri had recently shared the Gospel with our captain, and Andreas had placed his faith in Jesus as well. So Saul and Barnabas took advantage of the opportunity to teach him, as well as his crew, more about our Savior. By the time we docked in Salamis, the entire crew had come to believe!

Saul was overjoyed when he learned how many new Gentile believers had been added to the church in Salamis. Church leaders told us the believers were hungry to learn more but had many questions they could not answer. Saul and Barnabas decided to stay for a while so they could disciple the church and its elders. It also would give the two an opportunity to preach the Gospel in the local Jewish synagogues—something Saul had been unable to do on his previous visit.

Sadly, the Word of God fell on deaf ears in the synagogues. The men challenged Barnabas and Saul with questions but rejected their answers. It was contrary to the Gentiles who hungered to hear more. Barnabas and Saul soon sensed a release from the Spirit to concentrate on the Gentile believers exclusively.

We had been in Salamis about four weeks when Saul felt the Lord prompting us to move on. Saul and Barnabas preached from town to town as we made our way to the western side of the island. I marveled at how God had uniquely equipped the two of them.

Barnabas's encouraging nature put people at ease and created opportunities for Saul to present the Good News. Saul's prophetic nature provoked Barnabas to an even greater understanding of God's truths, which in turn enabled him to become a more effective encourager. God used each one's strengths and weaknesses to form an extremely gifted team.

I still wasn't sure what God's purpose was for my being on this journey when we arrived in Paphos. It had been more than twenty years since I had last seen my grandparents. Given the fact I had given them no forewarning of my arrival, they were, to say the least, surprised to find me and my traveling companions standing on their doorstep. It took them a few moments to recognize me.

Once they did, my grandmother let out a scream of delight and threw her arms around my neck. My grandfather was also happy to see me, just not quite as demonstrative.

"Welcome, John Mark!" my grandfather beamed. "And I see you have two friends traveling with you. Do my eyes deceive me, or is that you, Joseph?"

"It is most certainly, Andros!" Barnabas laughed. "Though all my friends now call me Barnabas. It is a pleasure to see you again after so many years. And this is our friend, Saul."

"Welcome to all of you," my grandmother said enthusiastically. "Please come into our home."

"How is your mother, John Mark?" my grandfather asked.

"The last I saw her she was doing well."

I explained I had been away from home for almost a year to travel with Barnabas and Saul.

"So both of you left your mother to attend to the business alone," my grandfather remarked, looking disappointedly at Barnabas and me.

"As you know, she is a most formidable woman," I replied. "It is she who suggested I travel with Barnabas and Saul. Mother assured me she and Mnason could more than adequately oversee the business—and I am certain it is not suffering from our absence."

"And I am certain you are correct!" Grandfather reluctantly acknowledged.

Our conversation quickly changed to the advance of the Gospel in Paphos, the capital city of Cyprus. Grandfather explained that after he returned home from being with us in Jerusalem twenty-two years ago, he had borne witness of the Good News of Jesus. Grandmother had been the first to believe, and others soon followed.

That small gathering of believers continued to grow, and the Holy Spirit led them in the truths of God's Word. "But we have needed men like you to come teach us more," Grandfather said, addressing Barnabas and Saul.

My grandfather invited the other believers in the community to gather in his home that night, and Saul and Barnabas began to teach them. Each night they returned with more friends in tow. By the third night, the gathering had spilled over into the street—and the crowd continued to multiply.

A few days later, Saul and Barnabas received an invitation from Sergius Paulus, the proconsul. He had heard about the growing crowds gathering to learn more about Jesus. Evidently, he wanted to hear the Word of God personally.

When we arrived at his home, the proconsul introduced us to a funny-looking little man, even shorter than Saul. His head bobbed up and down as he spoke in a shrill voice. He reminded me of one of those comical hand puppets used in Greek plays. But there was nothing comical about Elymas, a Jewish sorcerer.

Barnabas and Saul quickly recognized he was a false prophet sent by Satan to prevent the proconsul from accepting Jesus. Evidently, this magician had gained influence over the proconsul in the past; now, through his magic, his lies, and his interruptions, he was attempting to stop us from sharing the Good News.

"Pay no attention to what these men are saying, Proconsul," he boldly declared. "This man Saul has been imprisoned on more than one occasion for spreading his lies."

Saul looked the sorcerer in the eye and said, *"You son of the devil, full of every sort of deceit and fraud, and enemy of all that is good! Will you never stop perverting the true ways of the Lord? Watch now, for the Lord has laid His hand of punishment upon you, and you will be struck blind. You will not see the sunlight for some time."* [1]

The sorcerer instantly fell blind and began to wander about pleading for someone to take his hand and guide him. But the greater act of the Spirit of God was He opened the eyes of Sergius Paulus to the truth. When the proconsul saw what had happened, he immediately believed and asked that we teach him more about Jesus.

"I have heard stories about this Man, Jesus," he said. "But I thought they were just stories. Now I know the stories are true. He is the one true God, and from this day forward I will follow Him."

He then called for all his household to come and listen to Saul and Barnabas. Again, I stood amazed as the Holy Spirit spoke through both men. When they had finished sharing, the proconsul's family and staff also believed in Jesus.

The news of what happened to Elymas quickly spread throughout the city. A crowd assembled outside the proconsul's home as Saul and Barnabas stood on the roof and preached. Before the day was over, the proconsul, his household, and a multitude of others were baptized.

We remained in Paphos for two more weeks as Saul and Barnabas preached, discipled new believers, and trained church leaders. One night, Saul announced that the Spirit had told him it was time to go to Antioch of Pisidia.

The next day, the three of us said goodbye to my grandparents, as well as our many new brothers and sisters in Christ. We boarded a trading ship setting sail for a three-day journey to the port town of Perga in Pamphylia. The captain told us Perga was the ship's first destination. From there the ship would sail to Sidon, followed by Caesarea Maritima, and then return home to Paphos.

I perked up when the captain mentioned Caesarea Maritima, which wasn't too far from my home. Barnabas and Saul tried to engage the captain in conversation but realized neither he nor his crew was interested in hearing the Gospel. The two decided to spend their time below deck in extended prayer.

I remained on deck and pondered my situation. Though I was overjoyed about the activity of God during our time in Cyprus, I continued to wrestle with my purpose. I still felt responsibility as my father's heir to care for my mother and the family business. I knew I could continue to be a witness for Jesus through the business, so I did not see the two "callings" as mutually exclusive.

I realized Barnabas and Saul were well suited for a life of travel—neither had any family responsibilities. But I did. Surely God wanted me to honor those responsibilities; however, I also wanted to honor the commitment I had made to travel with Saul and Barnabas. Later that day, I approached Saul and, citing my reasons, told him I wanted to go home to Jerusalem.

I asked Saul when he thought we would return. He told me since the Spirit of God was leading us in our mission, we would trust His leadership and His time frame. So none of us had any idea when we might travel to Jerusalem. However, given the fact we had only recently departed from Antioch, Saul didn't expect it would be anytime soon. He reminded me of the task God had given us to take the Gospel to those who had not yet heard.

Though I understood what Saul was saying, it did not change my personal conviction. Given the unknown travel time, combined with the fact this ship was headed to Caesarea, I considered it a sign from the Holy Spirit that I was to remain on this ship.

When we arrived in Perga, I assisted Barnabas and Saul in finding a place to stay for the night. They did not know what was on my mind. Once they had settled in for the night, I penned a note:

Dear Saul and Barnabas,

"I am sorry to disappoint you both, but I have returned to the ship to continue my voyage to Caesarea Maritima. From there I will return to Jerusalem. I will pray that God grants you both favor as you carry on with the mission He has set before you."

Mark

18

A FORK IN THE ROAD

~

*T*he journey home gave me plenty of time to think about my decision to leave Barnabas and Saul. There were moments when I was certain I had made the right choice; but there were others when I felt like I was letting everyone down—Barnabas, Saul, my mother … even God!

By the time the ship arrived in Caesarea Maritima, I was thoroughly confused. As I made my way through the Judaean hills toward Jerusalem, I began to feel like I was the patriarch Jacob wrestling with the angel of the Lord at the Jabbok River.[1] But in my case, I couldn't seem to make peace with my decision.

My mother was surprised to see me back home. Her disappointment was obvious as I conveyed to her the manner in which I had deserted Barnabas and Saul. Her reaction caused me to question my choice even more.

As I settled back into life in Jerusalem, I learned that Peter had recently returned to the city. King Agrippa had been stricken with an illness and died soon after he executed James. Many people believed his death was due to his blasphemy of God when he permitted a delegation of people from Tyre and Sidon to flatter him to the point of worship. He had welcomed their adulation when they proclaimed him to be a god. It was a reminder that God will not share His glory.

With Agrippa dead, Emperor Claudius reestablished Roman governance and appointed Cuspius Fadus as procurator (governor). Fadus had no interest in persecuting the followers of Jesus. Accordingly, God orchestrated events to again place a hedge of protection around Peter and the other apostles. This left Peter free to return to Jerusalem without fear of repercussion.

I decided to seek his counsel regarding my conundrum.

"Peter, I stand at a fork in the road," I began. "One path leads me to take up the mantle left to me by my father as his only son. That means honoring him and my family's name by taking over leadership of the successful business he started. I was but a boy when he died, but I believe that is what he would want me to do.

"The other path is to live out the words Jesus spoke just before He ascended into the clouds—to be His witness to the ends of the world. I know I can be a witness as I lead my father's business; however, I believe the second path means devoting my life entirely to Christ—just as you, Barnabas, and Saul have done.

"My heart tells me to follow this second path, but my head tells me I am responsible for carrying forward my father's legacy. I have prayed, but I still do not know what to do. I feel like I'm back in the Garden of Gethsemane looking at Jesus. If I stay here and do my duty, I'll be abandoning Him all over again. But if I don't, I'll be abandoning my father. What should I do?"

"I cannot answer that for you, John Mark. All I can tell you is how I knew which path to take when I came to a similar fork in the road. I had taken over my deceased father's successful fishing business with his partner, Zebedee. He and I watched as his son John and my younger brother Andrew abandoned it all to follow Jesus. They left and never looked back.

"But I was wrestling with the same issue you are. I had people who depended on me: my wife, my daughters, and my partner. But when Jesus said to me, '*Come be My disciples, and I will show you how to fish for people,*'[2] I knew that is what I must do. I needed to trust Him to take care of my family and my business partner—and not look back."

I thought for a minute about what Peter said.

"The night my parents and I were baptized by you and the other disciples," I said thoughtfully, "Jesus told us we were to be the light of the world. We were not to hide the light under a basket. I know my father and mother both shined their light as they conducted business. However, if I stay here, I believe I will be hiding the light He has given me."

"In that case, John Mark," Peter replied, "I think you have your answer. If you do not go, you will be disobedient to the Holy Spirit's prompting. You must commit to Him all the other details, and trust Him to show you the right timing."

At that moment, all my doubts disappeared.

Two years passed as I waited for the right opportunity. One evening a familiar face appeared at our door. As delighted as I was to see him, I was also somewhat anxious. *How would he view me? How could he possibly forgive me?*

But Barnabas did not make me wait for an answer. He opened his arms and embraced me with the same genuine love he had always extended to me.

"John Mark, it is so good to see you again!" he declared. "I have looked forward to this moment ever since Paul and I knew we needed to return to Jerusalem."

"Paul?" I asked.

"Yes, Saul now goes by his Roman name since our ministry is primarily among Gentiles," Barnabas explained. "As a matter of fact, that change took place right after you left us in Perga."

An uncomfortable pause demanded that I bring things to a conclusion with my apology and explanation. I told Barnabas what I had been wrestling with while I was with them, and the thoughts I had when I decided to return home. I went on to explain what God had shown me since, including my conversation with Peter. Then I asked him to forgive me for deserting them and failing to honor my commitment.

"Peter was in Antioch a short time ago and told me what God has been doing in your life," Barnabas replied. "He tells me that he would take you on a journey without hesitation. That is partly why I have come to see you. There is a high probability that Paul and I will be traveling again soon to visit the new churches planted during our first trip. Would you be interested in joining us?"

"Yes, I would, without any doubt!" I declared hastily. "But is Paul willing for me to come along?"

"I will talk to him," Barnabas answered. "However, I wanted to know your response beforehand."

Mother joined us and we went on to talk about other things, including the main reason he and Paul had made this trip to Jerusalem.

"We have come to discuss the distinction that some of our leaders are making between our Gentile brothers and sisters and our Jewish believers. Some are advocating that Gentiles must first obey all the Laws of Moses before they can become followers of Jesus.

"But if we as Jews cannot walk in obedience to the laws, why would we shackle our Gentile brothers and sisters with that yoke? Paul and I have come to tell the group about the miraculous wonders we have seen God do among the Gentiles. God obviously makes no distinction between Jew and Gentile. His Spirit is at work in both to cleanse hearts and draw each one through faith to Himself.

"Church leaders must acknowledge that fact and not add burdens to these believers that Jesus has not."

In the days that followed, James and the other leaders came to that same conclusion. Paul's and Barnabas's efforts in Jerusalem had been successful, and it was time for them to return to Antioch. Before they departed, Barnabas and I visited once more.

"I will send word when it is time for you to come join us," he assured me.

～

19

DISAGREEMENTS THAT DIVIDE US

~

Several months later, I received the message from Barnabas I had been anticipating:

> Mark
> "Please convey my greetings to your mother and to the church meeting in your home. The time we discussed has come. Set out for Antioch as quickly as possible. Paul and I are planning to depart in three weeks. It will take a week for this message to make its way to you and another for you to travel here. So you must leave at once."
> Barnabas

He also included details about where I should meet them and a short list of items to bring with me from the Jerusalem church.

My mother and Mnason knew I would be leaving as soon as Barnabas sent word, so details related to managing the family business had already been addressed. Even the believers gathering in our home knew I intended to rejoin Paul and Barnabas. In many ways, I had already said my goodbyes, so I set out for Antioch the following morning.

Along the way, I rehearsed what I would say to Paul. He and I had not spoken when he and Barnabas were in Jerusalem. I was certain Barnabas had conveyed my deepest apologies, but I also was certain Paul had intentionally avoided me.

I did not want any awkwardness between us on this journey; I had been wrong and had learned from my ways. I would not abandon them again.

When I arrived in Antioch, I went straight to the location Barnabas had described. He greeted me warmly, but I noticed he looked uncomfortable.

"Is Paul here, or will he be joining us later?" I asked. "I have been rehearsing what I must say to him."

After a brief pause, Barnabas replied.

"No, Paul will not be joining us. He and I have decided to go our separate ways on this journey. You and I will sail to Cyprus to encourage the churches there, while Paul and someone else will visit the churches in Asia."

"Who will be accompanying Paul?" I asked earnestly. "And is this change because of me?"

"I do not yet know who will be joining Paul on his journey, but I do know that King Solomon wrote, *'We can make our plans, but the Lord determines our steps.'*[1] In His sovereignty, God has determined for us to part ways. We will entrust the outcome to Him."

"Yes, I understand," I replied. "But your message said I would be joining you *and* Paul. What happened to cause this change?"

Barnabas was making every effort to choose his words carefully, but finally he reluctantly told me, "Paul has not forgiven you for abandoning us in Perga. He was unwilling to take that chance with this trip. He said, 'The sake of the mission is too great! Our mandate to preach the Good News among the Gentiles of Asia and Europe cannot be put at risk.'"

"I understand why he feels that way," I responded. "But I had hoped for an opportunity to seek his forgiveness and convey the depth of my commitment. Is he unwilling to even speak with me?"

"Yes," Barnabas answered, "at this point he is still unwilling to sit down with you."

"Well," I said resignedly, "I must wait until another time to atone for my behavior. But why are you not going with him? Why must it be two journeys instead of one as originally planned?"

"Because I believe God is preparing you for great things, John Mark. As does Peter, I might add. I believe you *are* to make this journey—and if it is not to be with both Paul and me, then it must be with me alone.

"King Solomon also wrote, '*For everything there is a season, a time for every activity under heaven.*'[2] There is no question that our Lord has given Paul and me a season together—and He may again. But *this* season is for you and me to travel together."

I was sad that a rift had developed between these two good friends, and that I was the cause of it. But I, too, felt convicted to make this journey with Barnabas. I was excited to see what God was going to do in Cyprus *and* in Asia.

Two days later, Barnabas and I set sail. When we arrived in Salamis, we made our way to the home of brothers Andri and Tomys. Both men had become followers of Jesus through Paul's teaching. Tomys and Paul also shared an affinity that further strengthened their friendship—they were both tentmakers. Tomys had quickly demonstrated the ability to lead the new church in Salamis.

Tomys was delighted to see us and reported that the church had continued to increase daily over the past two years. After Tomys led a man named Hasan to the Lord, the new believer traveled to Paphos and joined my grandfather and other church leaders in spreading the Gospel. Now Tomys said a dozen more men had gone out to other places throughout Cyprus.

Barnabas and I remained in Salamis for several weeks to encourage and disciple believers. We learned that disagreements had occurred in the church between Gentile and Jewish believers, just as we had seen developing elsewhere.

Barnabas addressed the problem with church leaders.

"You must act in a way that promotes the unity of the Gospel with Jewish and Gentile believers alike; the church is a mixture of both. Since sharing meals as we fellowship has become a significant part of our gatherings, dietary practices have become troublesome between our two groups.

"However, God has not placed the burden of the law on Gentiles—and the Jews have no need to do so either. Jesus's blood was shed for Jew and

Gentile alike. One does not need to become like the other to partake in the grace of God. Rather, each needs to receive the gift of God by faith.

"I was recently in Jerusalem where Jesus's apostles discussed these very questions. After much prayer and consideration, they decided Gentile believers need to make some dietary concessions in deference to their Jewish brothers and sisters. Gentiles should abstain from eating blood or meat from animals that died by strangulation. This will promote unity within the body and present a united witness to a lost world. This compromise has already been put into practice by the believers in Antioch."

The leaders, Gentile and Jew alike, nodded their heads in agreement.

"These are reasonable concessions that we as Gentiles can make for the sake of unity within the body," declared the Gentile believers. The Jewish believers agreed: "We will not place on our Gentile brothers any burden that God has not put upon them."

"As Jesus told us, may we be known for the love we have for one another," Barnabas continued. "And may we do all we can to live in peace as we walk together with Him in His steps."

❧

20

NO MORE ABANDONMENT

~

For the next two years, we traveled from city to city along the island's eastern and southern coasts. The port cities of Kition, Amathus, and Kourion flourished under Roman rule as a result of increased trade with the rest of the empire. But the influx of Roman riches carried with it the worship of the Roman pagan gods, most notably Apollo Hylates.

The Gospel continued to spread, and the number of believers increased despite the burgeoning Roman religious influence. The minimal Jewish presence in these cities meant the churches were primarily Gentile believers. Though they were zealous in their faith, they were few in number and limited in their understanding of Scripture. The men sent by the church in Salamis to work in these cities had eventually become weary and discouraged.

Our work was not to unite Jewish and Gentile believers, but rather to add our voices to the preaching of the Gospel and to nurture, encourage, and equip leaders and other believers. I continued to learn from Barnabas's example of how best to minister to each individual's specific needs.

It was hard work—much harder than I had imagined. We knew the only way we would accomplish anything was through the work of the Holy Spirit. I learned more about depending on God's Spirit during those months in Cyprus than I had in all my prior years as a follower of Jesus.

God faithfully equipped and empowered us for any circumstances we encountered. We saw a renewed spirit in the leaders and believers in those cities, together with a fresh movement of His Spirit. To God be the praise and glory!

After more than a year on the island, we made our way to Paphos. The work there was thriving under the leadership of Hasan and the other elders of the church. Seeds that had been planted by my grandfather, as well as Paul and Barnabas, had produced a harvest that was continuing to multiply.

Sadly, I discovered that both my grandparents had declined physically since I last saw them. They were both bedridden, and even brief conversations required a great deal of effort from them. One week after we arrived, I watched my grandmother go to be with her Lord. The next day, my grandfather reunited with her in heaven.

I will eternally be grateful for two things in relation to their deaths. First, God graciously timed our arrival in Paphos so I could see my grandparents one last time. I was with them as they passed and had the chance to say goodbye. Second, God honored my grandfather's request that my grandmother not suffer the pain of losing him. And though he suffered the pain of losing her, it was only for a moment. As the psalmist wrote:

> *"Weeping may endure for a night,*
> *But joy comes in the morning."* [1]

In the days prior to his death, my grandfather passed along two things as part of his final blessing to me. First, he admitted that the best decision he ever made was not arguing with my mother about us returning to Paphos after my father's death.

"God intended for the two of you to be there," he said with determination. "He is doing great things in and through your life as a result of your being in Jerusalem. He enabled you to spend time with Jesus and allowed you to be discipled by the apostles and Barnabas. There is no doubt in my mind that He has great things in store for you in the days ahead. Continue to follow Him each and every step of the way."

Second, he told me he had already arranged for all of his business enterprises to pass to me upon his death.

"But do not be distracted or concerned about running the business," he said. "Allow your mother, and those she has put in place, to take care of it. You concentrate on the work God has placed before you, and allow her to concentrate on what He has placed before her."

I learned an important lesson from my grandfather: trust the people with whom God has surrounded you. Trust them to wisely use their gifts and talents. Grandfather demonstrated that trust by allowing my mother to lead his business and by his trust in Hasan to shepherd the church in Paphos.

Barnabas and I remained for several months before we sensed the Spirit leading us to return to Salamis. We set sail on Andri's merchant ship for our two-day journey.

When we arrived in Salamis, Tomys handed me a letter from Peter. Apparently, he had learned of my whereabouts through the church in Antioch. He invited me to come and assist him in Rome:

"John Mark,
Please come as soon as you can. You will be helpful to me in the ministry God has begun here. He prepared you in Cyprus for the work He has for you here in Rome.
Please do not delay.
May the Lord's grace be with you.
Peter"

When I showed the letter to Barnabas, I told him I had no intention of deserting him again. I would travel to Rome only if he released me to do so.

Without a moment of hesitation, he replied, "You will not be abandoning me, John Mark. God simply has another assignment for you. Peter is correct, the Lord has been preparing you for it. And now you must go in obedience.

"I also believe the Lord is directing me to bear witness to the Jews here in Salamis. So it is a change in direction for us both—and we must heed His voice.

"You are my cousin, John Mark, but you have become like a son to me. I am proud of who you have become in Christ. He has important work for you to do, and it is time for us to part ways."

Andri assisted me in making travel arrangements for a ship headed for Rome in a week. In the meantime, I assisted Tomys in teaching and training new believers in the church. Barnabas began to spend each day in one of the city's synagogues.

One night he told us, "Several men have arrived from Jerusalem. They continue to try to engage me in spirited debate about Jesus and the Scriptures. But the Spirit gives me the words to say and they are silenced—at least for a little while. However, I do not see them receiving my words; rather, they are more like the religious leaders who attempted to catch Jesus in their traps.

"Pray with me, John Mark, that the Spirit of God will continue to speak the truth through me."

I assured him I would and asked if he wanted me to join him the next day.

"No, we have our separate work to do. Gratefully, the Spirit of God goes with us both."

The next night, Barnabas did not return to Andri's home at his usual time. After several hours, we became concerned. Andri, Tomys, and I went looking for him. We visited the synagogues and all the places we thought he might be. Finally, we decided to look outside the city gates on the off chance he had gone there to pray.

It was there we found Barnabas . . . bloodied, beaten, and dead under a pile of rocks.

We cried out to the Lord in anguish. I immediately blamed myself.

"I should have gone with him today!" I bellowed between tears. "These men have done the same thing to him they did to Stephanos. They would not have risked stoning Barnabas if others had been with him. This is all my fault."

Tomys embraced me. "No, John Mark, it is not your fault. The Spirit of God was with Barnabas, just as He was with you. He is the One who ordered your steps today. He is the One who permitted this to occur. And now Barnabas is worshiping at the feet of Jesus!

"Can you imagine the joy he is experiencing this very minute? Would you desire to rob him of that and bring him back to this place? No, John Mark, you were not meant to be with him. His work was completed. God has more for you to do on this side of heaven. Allow Him to comfort you in your sorrow."

Though I knew Tomys's words were true, it took a while for them to work their way into my heart. I will miss my cousin until the day we are reunited. But I did come to accept that I had not abandoned him . . . and he had not abandoned me.

Two days later, I set sail for Rome.

〰

21

ROME

~

Though Rome was primarily a pagan city—filled with reminders of the worship of false gods—it prided itself on being "welcoming" to all religions. There were even several Jewish synagogues in the city.

Before I arrived, Peter had endeavored to teach in those synagogues without success. Even in Rome, he was well-known among the Jewish leaders as having been one of Jesus's closest disciples and one whom the high council in Jerusalem had deemed a threat to Judaism. They considered his teaching, just as they had the teaching of Jesus, to be destructive to their positions and authority.

However, the Lord enabled Peter and me to openly preach the Gospel elsewhere throughout Rome, and we saw many Gentiles come to faith. A church was soon established and began to flourish as people from all walks of life accepted Christ.

During the countless hours Peter and I were together, he shared his personal account of the ministry, crucifixion, and resurrection of Jesus. These conversations reminded me of previous accounts I had been told by others during my time in the Jerusalem church.

One day as he was sharing one of his memories, Peter challenged me with the idea of the need for a written account of Jesus's story. He told me he believed I was one of the men the Lord had chosen to record it. To our knowledge, it would be the first written account about Jesus. After Peter left Rome to go to Corinth, I remained in the city to nurture new believers and leaders, and to complete the writing task he had given me.

Soon after I finished writing, I was surprised to learn that Paul was in Rome! He was under house arrest but was allowed to have visitors. I received the news from a new follower by the name of Pontius Aquila. He was an officer in the Praetorian guard, an elite unit within the Roman army, stationed in Rome.

Aquila and his mother, Claudia, had recently been baptized by a man named Aristarchus. Aquila told me that Aristarchus was one of the travel companions who had arrived in Rome with Paul.

Though I was taken aback about Paul's presence in the city, I was even more astounded when Aquila told me his story.

"I understand that you are from Jerusalem, John Mark. In that case, you are very familiar with my father, Pontius Pilate, who served as the prefect of the Iudaean province for several years.

"I spent my youth in the palace in Caesarea Maritima," Aquila told me. "My mother and I were both in Jerusalem when the religious leaders brought Jesus of Nazareth before my father. I watched from the roof as my father condemned Jesus to die on the cross. My father knew He was innocent, and so did my mother and I.

"We cried as we watched my father refuse to stand up to the crowd for what was right. I was ashamed as he ceremoniously washed his hands. It was a turning point in my life. Until that moment, I would have followed my father anywhere.

"When the soldiers led Jesus to the cross, I covered myself with a cloak and followed from a distance. I watched as He was crucified under my father's order. I knew He was not only an innocent Man, falsely accused, but my mother and I also knew He was a righteous Man. I later heard He had risen from the grave, though my father denied the reports. He contended that Jesus's disciples had moved His body. But I never believed that."

Aquila began to weep as he continued. "My mother and I have waited for over thirty years to hear the rest of the story, and yesterday Paul told us! My father died ten years ago, never knowing the complete truth, but my mother and I are now followers of Jesus."

I told Aquila how my mother and I had seen Jesus the night of His resurrection, and how we had been there the day He ascended into heaven. "Actually, I have just completed a written account of His ministry, crucifixion, and resurrection. Would you like to read it?"

I watched Aquila's face light up as Jesus's story unfolded before his eyes. I also saw his pain as he remembered the role his father had played in Jesus's death. But he could not contain his excitement when he read the details of Christ's resurrection.

After he finished reading, I asked him if he might be able to arrange for me to visit Paul. "Of course I can," he replied. "We will go see him in the morning!"

Paul was caught off guard when Aquila and I walked into his room. It was a moment that was long overdue. I asked his forgiveness for the way I had abandoned him in Perga. He sought my forgiveness for the ill-will he had harbored against me.

Paul knew about Barnabas's and my work in Cyprus, but he was unaware of Barnabas's death. He was distraught when I relayed the details of the stoning. He told me he regretted how he and Barnabas had parted company. However, I reminded him that Barnabas never held any malice. He had always known that God had a plan for all of us—that did not include the three of us making that second journey together.

"God used the two of you to spread the Gospel in Cyprus," Paul said. "And he used you and Peter to spread it here in Rome. To God be the glory!"

When I told him about my chronicle detailing Jesus's life, he asked me to read it aloud. He was surprised that I had been present in the garden the night Jesus was arrested. I explained that I rarely shared that story because I was ashamed that I had abandoned Jesus. He then graciously reminded me I was not the only one who had ever abandoned Jesus!

Everyone in the room listened intently as I read the account of Jesus's life. One of Paul's traveling companions—the physician Luke, whom I had met in Antioch—listened the most carefully. He desired to record the events surrounding the birth of the church, and Paul encouraged him to do so. It became clear we would become collaborators in capturing the truths and events of the Gospel message.

It wasn't long before another of Paul's travel companions, Timothy, arrived along with many others. However, eventually only Luke, Aristarchus, Timothy, and I remained with Paul, as did our Roman brothers and sisters.

Paul remained under house arrest for two years. Throughout that time, his accusers from Jerusalem never made an appearance. He could not be granted an appointment to appeal before the emperor if there was no one to make a charge. So, Pontius Aquila and others appealed to the prefect for his release, and it was granted. Paul hadn't been given the opportunity to proclaim the Good News to the emperor, as he had hoped, but the Spirit gave him the chance to preach to many others—some of whom may share it with the emperor one day.

Luke and Aristarchus set off with Paul for Macedonia. Timothy headed for Ephesus and I journeyed to Antioch to join Simon Peter. The Spirit gave each of us a peace that our work in Rome was done—at least for now. The Lord had raised up strong believers, like Aquila, to lead the work.

Eventually, the Lord led Peter to go to Corinth, before later prompting him to return to Rome. Soon after Peter's arrival, a fire broke out in one of the cook shops along the side of the Circus Maximus. It was a windy day, and the fire spread quickly. It took nine days before it could be contained.

The fire destroyed a substantial part of the city, leaving many dead and many others homeless. The surviving citizens of Rome were irate with Emperor Nero. Why had he not led the city to react more quickly to extinguish the flames? There were some who said he had set the fire himself.

The emperor immediately took action to divert the blame elsewhere. Someone within his inner circle suggested the Christians. Nero favored the idea and announced Christians were a threat to the empire. He accused us of being troublemakers who followed a leader who was crucified for His acts of rebellion. He told the entire empire that Christians needed to be purged before they destroyed everything. He sent out troops to arrest followers of Jesus. By then there were Christian brothers in the senate and the military who attempted to reason with him, but he would not listen.

He began having Christians crucified on the streets of Rome as a spectacle for the city. When he was informed that one of Jesus's apostles was in the city, he sent soldiers to apprehend Peter. There was no trial. Nero had him crucified immediately. However, Peter told his executioners he was unworthy to be crucified in the same manner as his Savior, so he hung on the cross upside down as he requested.

Soon thereafter, Paul was arrested in Troas and taken in chains back to Rome. This time he wasn't under house arrest, and neither was he permitted any visitors other than Luke and Aristarchus. He sent a letter to Timothy with this request:

"Timothy, my dear son,

Please come as soon as you can. Bring John Mark with you when you come, for he will be helpful to me in my ministry. I am sending Tychicus to you, so he can continue the work while you are gone. When you come, be sure to bring the coat I left with Carpus at Troas. Also bring my books, and especially my papers. Do your best to get here before winter.

May the Lord be with your spirit. And may His grace be with all of you."(3)

Timothy and I never made that journey. Just prior to our departure, we learned that Paul had been executed. He was now in the presence of his beloved Savior.

As the years pass, I frequently think about the three men who were so instrumental in my life—Barnabas, Peter, and Paul. I imagine the three of them kneeling together at the feet of Jesus. They fought the good fight.

They finished the race. They kept the faith.[2] I pray that each of us follows in their steps.

PLEASE HELP ME BY LEAVING A REVIEW!

i would be very grateful if you would leave a review of this book. Your feedback will be helpful to me in my future writing endeavors and will also assist others as they consider picking up a copy of the book.

To leave a review:

Go to: amazon.com/dp/195686637X

Or scan this QR code using your camera on your smartphone:

Thanks for your help!

∽

YOU WILL WANT TO READ ALL THE BOOKS IN "THE CALLED" SERIES

Stories of these ordinary men and women called by God to be used in extraordinary ways.

A Carpenter Called Joseph (Book 1)

A Prophet Called Isaiah (Book 2)

A Teacher Called Nicodemus (Book 3)

A Judge Called Deborah (Book 4)

A Merchant Called Lydia (Book 5)

A Friend Called Enoch (Book 6)

A Fisherman Called Simon (Book 7)

A Heroine Called Rahab (Book 8)

A Witness Called Mary (Book 9)

A Cupbearer Called Nehemiah (Book 10)

A Follower Called Mark (Book 11)

A Psalmist Called Asaph (Book 12) - Coming soon

AVAILABLE IN PAPERBACK, LARGE PRINT, AND FOR KINDLE ON AMAZON.

ALSO, A **DISCUSSION GUIDE** IS AVAILABLE AS A RESOURCE **FOR YOUR SMALL GROUP OR BOOK CLUB** AS YOU DISCUSS EACH OF THE BOOKS. AVAILABLE ON AMAZON IN PRINT OR FOR YOUR KINDLE.

Scan this QR code using your camera on your smartphone to see the entire series.

"THE PARABLES" SERIES

An Elusive Pursuit (Book 1)

Twenty-three year old Eugene Fearsithe boarded a train on the first day of April 1912 in pursuit of his elusive dream. Little did he know where the journey would take him, or what . . . and who . . . he would discover along the way.

Available on Amazon

A Belated Discovery (Book 2)

Nineteen year old Bobby Fearsithe enlisted in the army on the fifteenth day of December 1941 to fight for his family, his friends, and his neighbors. Along the way, he discovered just who his neighbor truly was.

Available on Amazon

AVAILABLE IN HARDCOVER, PAPERBACK, LARGE PRINT, AUDIO, AND FOR KINDLE ON AMAZON.

Scan this QR code using your camera on your smartphone to see the entire series.

For more information, go to *kenwinter.org* or *wildernesslessons.com*

ALSO BY KENNETH A. WINTER

THROUGH THE EYES
(a series of biblical fiction novels)

Through the Eyes of a Shepherd (Shimon, a Bethlehem shepherd)
Through the Eyes of a Spy (Caleb, the Israelite spy)
Through the Eyes of a Prisoner (Paul, the apostle)

❧

THE EYEWITNESSES
(a series of biblical fiction short story collections)

For Christmas/Advent

Little Did We Know – the advent of Jesus — for adults
Not Too Little To Know – the advent – ages 8 thru adult

For Easter/Lent

The One Who Stood Before Us – the ministry and passion of Jesus — for adults
The Little Ones Who Came – the ministry and passion – ages 8 thru adult

❧

LESSONS LEARNED IN THE WILDERNESS SERIES
(a non-fiction series of biblical devotional studies)

The Journey Begins (Exodus) – Book 1
The Wandering Years (Numbers and Deuteronomy) – Book 2
Possessing The Promise (Joshua and Judges) – Book 3
Walking With The Master (The Gospels leading up to Palm Sunday) – Book 4
Taking Up The Cross (The Gospels – the passion through ascension) – Book 5
Until He Returns (The Book of Acts) – Book 6

ALSO AVAILABLE AS AUDIOBOOKS

THE CALLED series

A Carpenter Called Joseph

A Prophet Called Isaiah

A Teacher Called Nicodemus

A Judge Called Deborah

A Merchant Called Lydia

A Friend Called Enoch

A Fisherman Called Simon

A Heroine Called Rahab

A Witness Called Mary

A Cupbearer Called Nehemiah

A Follower Called Mark

❧

THROUGH THE EYES series

Through the Eyes of a Shepherd

Through the Eyes of a Spy

Through the Eyes of a Prisoner

❧

Little Did We Know

Not Too Little to Know

❧

THE PARABLES series

An Elusive Pursuit

A Belated Discovery

❧

SCRIPTURE BIBLIOGRAPHY

~

The basis for the story line of this book is taken from the Gospel according to Mark and the Acts of the Apostles in the Holy Bible. Certain fictional events or depictions of those events have been added.

Some of the dialogue in this story are direct quotations from Scripture. Here are the specific references for those quotations:

Chapter 1

[1] Mark 14:45

[2] Luke 22:48

[3] Luke 22:51; Matthew 26:52-53

Chapter 3

[1] John 2:16

[2] John 2:19-20

[3] John 2:19

Chapter 4

[1] John 1:36

Chapter 5

[1] Mark 9:37

[2] Matthew 5:14-16

Chapter 8

[1] John 3:16

Chapter 9

[1] Based upon Jesus's statements in Mark 10:30 and John 3:16-17

[2] Based upon Jeremiah 29:11

[3] Mark 11:9-10

Chapter 10

[1] Mark 11:17, quoting Isaiah 56:7 and Jeremiah 7:11

[2] Matthew 21:15

[3] Matthew 21:16

[4] Matthew 21:16, quoting Psalm 8:2

Chapter 11

[1] Mark 16:6

[2] John 20:19

[3] Mark 16:15-16

Chapter 12

(1) Acts 2:13

(2) Acts 2:14-16

(3) Acts 2:17-21 quoting Joel 2:28-32

(4) Acts 4:19-20

(5) Acts 4:29-30

(6) Acts 5:3-4

(7) Acts 5:7

(8) Acts 5:7

(9) Acts 5:9

Chapter 13

(1) Acts 5:41

(2) Acts 5:20

(3) Acts 5:28

(4) Acts 5:29-32

(5) Acts 7:51-53

(6) Acts 7:56

(7) Acts 7:59

(8) Acts 7:60

Chapter 14

(1) Ephesians 3:8

Chapter 16

(1) Acts 12:14

(2) Acts 12:15

(3) Acts 13:2

Chapter 17

[1] Acts 13:10-11

Chapter 18

[1] For context read Genesis 32:22-26

[2] Mark 1:17

Chapter 19

[1] Proverbs 16:9

[2] Ecclesiastes 3:1

Chapter 20

[1] Psalm 30:5 (NKJ)

Chapter 21

[1] 2 Timothy 4:9, 11-13, 22

[2] 2 Timothy 4:7

❧

LISTING OF CHARACTERS
(ALPHABETICAL ORDER)

～

Many of the characters in this book are real people pulled directly from the pages of Scripture. I have not changed any details about a number of those individuals except the addition of their interactions with the fictional characters. They are noted below as "UN" (unchanged).

In other instances, fictional details have been added to real people to provide backgrounds about their lives where Scripture is silent. The intent is that you understand these were real people, whose lives were full of all of the many details that fill our own lives. They are noted as "FB" (fictional background).

In some instances, we are never told the names of certain individuals in the Bible. In those instances, where i have given them a name as well as a fictional background, they are noted as "FN" (fictional name).

Lastly, a number of the characters are purely fictional, added to convey the fictional elements of these stories. They are noted as "FC" (fictional character).

～

Agabus – a prophet from Jerusalem (UN)
Ananias – believer in Damascus who discipled Saul (UN)

Ananias – husband of Saphira, member of Jerusalem church who lied about gift (UN)

Andreas – Cypriot ship captain (FC)

Andrew – son of Jonah, brother of Simon Peter, apostle of Jesus (FB)

Andri – Cypriot ship captain, brother of Tomys (FC)

Andros – father of Damaris, grandfather of John Mark (FC)

Annas – high priest (6 - 15 AD) (UN)

Aristarchus – early believer in Thessalonica, companion of Paul (FB)

Artemis – Cypriot ship's captain (FC)

Aurelius – Christian in Antioch killed in earthquake (FC)

Barnabas/Joseph – cousin of John Mark, nephew of Mary (John Mark's mother), cousin of Mnason, co-laborer with Saul/ Paul (FB)

Bartholomew – apostle of Jesus (UN)

Caiaphas – high priest (18 - 36 AD) (UN)

Carpus - the one with whom the apostle Paul left his cloak (UN)

Claudia – wife of Pontius Pilate, mother of Pontius Aquila (FB)

Cuspius Fadus – Roman procurator of Iudaean province (UN)

Damaris – son of Andros, husband of Mary, father of John Mark (FC)

Elymas – Jewish sorcerer in Paphos (UN)

Emperor Augustus – ruled Roman Empire 27 BC - 14 AD (UN)

Emperor Caligula – ruled Roman Empire 37 - 41 AD (UN)

Emperor Claudius – ruled Roman Empire 41 - 54 AD (UN)

Emperor Nero – ruled Roman Empire 54 - 68 AD (UN)

Emperor Tiberius – ruled Roman Empire 14 - 37 AD (UN)

Gamaliel – rabbi, grandson of Hillel (FB)

Hasan – Agagite prime minister of Persia under Xerxes (UN)

Herod Agrippa – puppet king who ruled Iudaea (41 - 44 A.D.) (UN)

Herod Antipas – 6th son of Herod the Great, ethnarch over Galilee and Perea (UN)

Herod the Great – the tetrarch (UN)

Hillel – the Elder, a respected teacher, grandfather of Gamaliel (UN)

Jacob – also called Israel, patriarch of the Jews, son of Isaac (UN)

James – son of Joseph & Mary, half-brother of Jesus, leader of Jerusalem church (FB)

James – son of Zebedee, brother of John, apostle of Jesus (UN)

James (the Less) – apostle of Jesus, cousin of Jesus, brother of Thaddeus (FB)

Jesus of Nazareth – the Son of God (UN)

Joel – Old Testament prophet (UN)

John – son of Zebedee, brother of James, apostle of Jesus (FB)

John Mark – son of Damaris and Mary, colaborer with Barnabas, Paul, and Peter (FB)

John the baptizer – son of Zechariah (UN)

Jonah - father of Simon Peter and Andrew (UN)

Joseph of Arimathea – pharisee, follower of Jesus (FB)

Judas Iscariot – the betrayer (UN)

King Solomon – 3rd king of Israel, son of King David (UN)

Lucius – Jew from Cyrene, cousin of Simon the Cyrene, elder of church at Antioch (FB)

Luke – the physician, travel companion of Paul, Gospel writer (FB)

Malchus – servant to Caiaphas whose ear was cut off at Gethsemane (FB)

Manaen – Essene who grew up in Herod's palace, elder of church at Antioch (FB)

Martha – servant in Mary's home in Jerusalem (FC)

Mary – aunt of Jesus, mother of James (the Less) and Thaddeus (UN)

Mary – mother of John Mark, aunt of Barnabas (FB)

Mnason – cousin of Barnabas, friend of Saul, employed by Mary (FB)

Nicodemus – rabbi in Capernaum, pharisee, follower of Jesus (FB)

Philip – fisherman, apostle of Jesus (UN)

Pontius Aquila II (aka Aquila) – son of Pontius Pilate & Claudia, witness of Jesus's crucifixion, member of Roman senate, friend of Paul (FC)

Pontius Pilate – Roman prefect of Judea (UN)

Rhoda – servant of Mary (UN)

Rufus – Christian in Antioch killed in earthquake (FC)

Salome – wife of Zebedee, mother of James and John (UN)

Saphira – wife of Ananias, member of Jerusalem church who lied about gift (UN)

Saul/Paul – persecutor of believers, follower of Jesus, apostle to the Gentiles (FB)

Sergio Paulus – proconsul of Paphos (UN)

Shimon – the shepherd, disciple of John the baptizer, disciple of Jesus (FC)

Simeon – Gentile from Nubia, elder of church at Antioch (FB)

Simon (Peter) – son of Jonah, husband of Gabriella, apostle of Jesus (FB)

Simon the Cyrene – man who carried the cross of Jesus (UN)

Simon the zealot – apostle of Jesus (FB)

Stephanos – Hellenistic Jew chosen by early church to serve widows (FB)

Thaddeus – apostle of Jesus, cousin of Jesus, brother of James (the Less) (FB)

Timothy – companion of Paul from Lystra (UN)

Tomys – brother of Andri, tentmaker, leader of church in Salamis (FC)

Tychicus – believer from Ephesus, traveled with Paul (UN)
Unnamed captain of ship that carried John Mark back to Paphos (FC)
Unnamed cook on the Kyrenia (FC)
Unnamed crippled child in Jerusalem (FC)
Unnamed father of crippled child in Jerusalem (FC)
Unnamed wife of Andros - mother of Damaris, grandmother of John Mark (FC)
Yitzhak – the tradesman who owned the upper room (FC)
Zafer – Cypriot ship's helmsman (FC)
Zebedee – father of James and John (UN)

ACKNOWLEDGMENTS

I do not cease to give thanks for you ….
Ephesians 1:16 (ESV)

… my partner and best friend, LaVonne,
for choosing to trust God as we walk together with Him in this faith
adventure;

… my family,
for your continuing love, support and encouragement;

… Sheryl,
for your partnership in the work;

… Scott,
for using the gifts God has given you;

… a wonderful group of advance readers,
who encourage and challenge me in the journey;

… and most importantly,
the One who goes before me in all things
– my Lord and Savior Jesus Christ!

∾

FROM THE AUTHOR

A word of explanation for those of you who are new to my writing.

You will notice that whenever i use the pronoun "I" referring to myself, i have chosen to use a lowercase "i." This only applies to me personally (in the Preface). i do not impose my personal conviction on any of the characters in this book. It is not a typographical error. i know this is contrary to proper English grammar and accepted editorial style guides. But years ago, the Lord convicted me – personally – that in all things i must decrease and He must increase. And as a way of continuing personal reminder, from that day forward, i have chosen to use a lowercase "i" whenever referring to myself.

Because of the same conviction, i use a capital letter for any pronoun referring to God. The style guide for most translations of Scripture do not share that conviction. However, you will see that i have intentionally made that slight revision and capitalized any pronoun referring to God in any quotations of Scripture. Please accept my apology for any style guide violations , but i must honor this conviction.

Lastly, regarding this matter – this is a <u>personal</u> conviction – and i share it only so you will understand why i have chosen to deviate from normal editorial practice. i am in no way suggesting or endeavoring to have anyone else subscribe to my conviction. Thank you for your under-standing.

~

ABOUT THE AUTHOR

Ken Winter is a follower of Jesus, an extremely blessed husband, and a proud father and grandfather – all by the grace of God. His journey with Jesus has led him to serve on the pastoral staffs of two local churches – one in West Palm Beach, Florida and the other in Richmond, Virginia – and as the vice president of mobilization of an international missions organization.

Today, Ken continues in that journey as a full-time author, teacher and speaker. You can read his weekly blog posts at kenwinter.blog and listen to his weekly podcast at kenwinter.org/podcast.

And we proclaim Him, admonishing every man and teaching every man with all wisdom, that we may present every man complete in Christ. And for this purpose also I labor, striving according to His power, which mightily works within me.
(Colossians 1:28-29 NASB)

PLEASE JOIN MY READERS' GROUP

Please join my Readers' Group in order to receive updates and information about future releases, etc.

Also, i will send you a free copy of *The Journey Begins* e-book — the first book in the *Lessons Learned In The Wilderness* series. It is yours to keep or share with a friend or family member that you think might benefit from it.

It's completely free to sign up. i value your privacy and will not spam you. Also, you can unsubscribe at any time.

Go to kenwinter.org to subscribe.

Or scan this QR code using your camera on your smartphone:

∽

www.ingramcontent.com/pod-product-compliance
Lightning Source LLC
Chambersburg PA
CBHW051846170626
46807CB00003B/1370